THE MYSTERY OF
SUNDAYS WELL

Murder in a small Irish town

ANNE CROSSE

THE
BOOK
FOLKS

Paperback published by The Book Folks

London, 2019

ISBN 978-1-0827-0894-7

www.thebookfolks.com

For my three sons: Colin, Shaun and Alan.

CHAPTER 1

Councillor John Hanton studied his reflection in the bathroom mirror. He had come a long way from the days of being subjected to jibes and taunts, because nowadays everyone doffed their caps when they saw him coming. He was so proud of the many battles he had bravely fought and won, so proud of his well-deserved status. He was the most important person in Magnerstown, and by God he had earned it.

If only his mother was alive to witness the success of this fatherless child. She would be so proud of him. You have turned into one hell of a handsome devil, she would say, and we did it all on our own without that cad.

The buzzing of the doorbell broke in on his thoughts.

His special mission this morning was to attend a photo session just outside town. Work had started on the refurbishment of the area, and the local newspaper *The Crier* would be doing an article on how he had single-handedly managed to get funding to turn Sundays Well into a tourist attraction.

He was the hero of the hour, even if he said so himself, and the businessmen who had up until now looked down their noses at him, were scrambling to be seen in his company. As a result of this venture, money would pour into the town, which had become a shadow of its former self; money that was, according to a committee set up by a group of the townspeople, badly needed for its survival.

Martin Hayes greeted him when he answered the door. "John, I hope you don't mind me calling, but they are all waiting for you."

John looked at his watch. "I'm so sorry but I thought…"

"We brought the time forward, didn't your wife tell you?" Martin asked.

John flushed with fury. She had done it on purpose, the witch, probably because she wanted to take the car to go off on some mad hare-brained scheme of hers. Oh, he would give her such a right rollicking tonight. "Just let me get my coat," he said.

"I'll drive you out." Martin made the offer when he noted the absence of the counsellor's black Mercedes Benz in the driveway.

"Just give me a minute and I will be with you," John said.

Martin slipped into the seat of his humble, battered Jeep. He would love to tell Councillor John Hanton what he thought of the whole stupid idea. Revamping the old well was laughable. The right thing to do would be to knock the thing down, cover the blooming thing in, and build a new one altogether. It would be cheaper and quicker. But no, we have now entered the age of 'preserve our heritage' and all that new historical nonsense. "Heritage, my arse," Martin growled. He flicked his cigarette out the window when the man of the moment plonked his bony arse down onto the passenger seat beside him.

As Martin drove out to the site, he tuned out from the counsellor babbling beside him.

How the hell this gimpy geek managed to get a wife for himself, was an absolute mystery. Her name was Ella and she was a nice woman, he'd been told. Taking a quick sideways glance at the excuse for a man sitting beside him, Martin felt extreme sympathy for the woman who had to share a bed with him.

"Here we are." John stated the obvious as they arrived on site.

One of the workmen ran up to Martin as soon as he stepped out of the Jeep. "There's something down in the well. Mick McCarthy is checking it out."

Martin walked over to the well and leaned over the edge.

"Come up at once, Mick!" Martin shouted. Health and safety would have his guts for garters if the man came a cropper.

"It's foul," Mick announced as he emerged from the well.

"Birds is it, or chickens?" Martin said.

"Not that kind of fowl," Mick replied.

"I was only joking, Mick. Now get out of my way," Martin ordered.

Martin climbed down the ladder armed with a torch and a stick. He would have to see for himself exactly what was going on because Mick was inclined to be a bit of a drama queen. He knew that from past experiences. He was certain all he would find down there would be a few flying rats – crows, in other words.

Joey Tyrell felt a fluttering in his chest. He had a premonition to bring his very best camera with him today, and his premonitions were always well founded. There hadn't been breaking news in town since the murders two years ago, and he somehow had a feeling in his waters that something big was about to go down.

Martin shone his torch around the small confines of the well. He could just about make out a few rags.

3

He poked the stick into the middle of the rags and felt something hard. He rummaged around and felt other items, like sticks or something. Then something bigger.

A blackened head leered up at him. Dropping the torch like it was a hot potato, Martin scuttled up the ladder without looking back.

"Well, boss," Joey Tyrell drawled, "is it a case of ding dong bell, there's a pussy in the well?"

"Is everything going well in the well?" Councillor Hanton laughed.

Everyone stared at the counsellor blankly.

"Well, do you get it? It's a pun," the councillor said, sniggering.

"You are a right comedian." Joey Tyrell humoured him.

"Sure, isn't the whole town laughing at him?" Martin managed to sound normal even though he was feeling far from it.

Everyone laughed at Martin's remark, giving him the cue to move off to the side of the road. With a shaky hand, he punched in the number of the local Garda station. Why he was even bothering making the call, he didn't know. All that was up there now in the two-bit station was one desk sergeant and a young one doing the paperwork.

"Hello, Magnerstown Garda station," the voice at the other end announced.

Martin couldn't help thinking that this feeble exercise would be like going into a hardware store and asking for a pint of milk.

"There's something in Sundays Well," Martin said.

"Water, is it?" the desk sergeant asked.

"Oh fuck off!" Martin snapped.

"Sorry, do go on," the desk sergeant said.

"A skeleton," Martin said.

"Right, leave it with me," the desk sergeant answered.

Martin switched his phone off and almost collided with Joey Tyrell who had crept up behind him.

"Ding dong bell, there is a pussy in the well." Joey smiled.

CHAPTER 2

Detective Inspector Robert Carroll searched his pockets in vain for the cigarette butt he had carefully wrapped in a tissue.

Martin Hayes produced a packet of cigarettes, took one out, and handed it to Robert. "I presume that's what you want," he said.

"Thanks," Robert said gratefully. "I just got here an hour ago and I'm not quite settled in yet."

"From the big smoke, are you?" Martin asked.

"Yeah, from the big smoke to the sticks, and before you say it, yes I am badly in need of this smoke," Robert replied.

"Population five thousand, four hundred and twenty-two, and the killer is amongst them," Martin said as he handed over his lighter.

Robert coughed after taking a drag.

"Strong, eh? I buy them from a Polish lad who runs Cliff's Restaurant."

"I'd imagine he'd need the sideline. Shouldn't think Cliff is paying him much," Robert said with a snarl.

"Sorry I'm late, sir."

Robert turned to face the long-haired young man and made a huge effort to sound sincere. "James, we meet again," he said.

James held out his hand to Martin. "I'm James Sayder," he said.

Not wanting to be left out, Robert introduced himself too.

"And I'm the Queen of Sheba." Martin laughed.

"And pussy's in the well," Robert grinned.

"Not quite right, there were two bodies in the well, and they've been moved to the hospital mortuary," Martin said.

"Nothing should have been removed until I... I mean, we got here," Robert admonished.

"Any idea who they are?" James intervened.

"One dead head is the same as the next," Martin said, and laughed.

"You find this amusing, do you?" Robert asked.

"There hasn't been a murder in this town for a while now. That's what I've been told by the photographer from the local newspaper," Martin said.

"Murder, you say." Robert blew smoke into the air.

"They hardly threw themselves in," Martin said in defence.

"Who threw them in, little Tommy? Can never remember his name," James said.

Robert fixed James with a look and scowled. "Enough of this frivolity."

"Sorry, sir."

"It was Thin, little Tommy Thin," Martin said. "My mother was a great one for the nursery rhymes."

"Yes, you are right, it was Tommy Thin," James said.

"Who pulled him out, little Tommy Stout?" Martin said.

"It was indeed," James agreed.

"I said enough..."

"Sorry, sir," James said.

"Best thing we can do now is head back to the hotel, James, because I'm starving," Robert said.

"Shouldn't we check into the Garda station first?" James asked.

Robert stubbed out the remainder of the cigarette underfoot and strode off in the direction of the road. "All in good time," he called over his shoulder.

"Do you two not want a lift back to the hotel?" Martin asked.

"It's only a ten-minute walk, the air will do us good." Robert gestured to James, who dutifully followed.

* * *

Robert put his knife and fork down. "So, what room did they put you in, James?" he asked.

"Number twenty-two, sir."

"I'm next door then."

"In twenty-three?"

"Twenty-one."

"It's nice here, isn't it?" James remarked.

"I hate hotels," Robert said.

"Could you not have stayed in Forge Cottage, sir? Sorry, shouldn't have asked, it's none of my business."

"She, I mean Maggie Lehane…"

"To give the woman her full title," James interrupted.

"She has allowed Mossie Harrington to take up residence there."

"You mean the fellow who works for her?"

"Yes, *The Crier's* printer, or compositor or whatever they call themselves nowadays," Robert said.

"Is he house-sitting, then?"

"Apparently he was turfed out of his own house."

"Why?"

The pretty young receptionist smiled at James rather than at Robert. "Excuse me for interrupting your breakfast," she said.

James smiled back.

8

She turned her attention to Robert. "A message for you," she said.

"What is it?" Robert asked.

"Doctor Morris called last night, and he left a message for you."

"Is that old goat still around?"

"He said he'll be carrying out the autopsy."

"Here we go again," Robert said.

"That's the number you can contact him at." The receptionist handed a small envelope to Robert and quickly turned on her heels.

James laughed inwardly. When he first met Robert Carroll two years ago, he immediately came to the conclusion that he had just met the most bad-tempered person one could ever meet, and the man hadn't changed on that score. He was still rubbing people up the wrong way, but apart from that, he had to admit, if only to himself, he liked Robert Carroll despite all his faults.

"So, what happened between you and your little nurse friend, Katie; wasn't that her name?" Robert asked.

"She's gone off to Australia. She is doing some kind of medical course. But, to be honest…"

"Going a bit stale, was it?" Robert interjected.

"And you, sir, how are things going between you and Maggie Lehane?" James couldn't believe he had actually asked Robert that question.

"She got herself a job for a newspaper in London, and she couldn't wait to get on the plane. In fact, now that I think of it, she ran up the runway like she was being chased by a dragon."

"I never thought she'd leave *The Crier*," James said.

"That beardy photographer fellow who was snapping away out at Sundays Well today, Joey fucking whatever he is called, and that Mossie Harrington jack of all trades idiot fellow are both running the show now."

"From the horse's mouth you got that information? Not that I am calling Maggie Lehane a horse, you understand," James said.

"No, it was the builder Martin Hayes who told me," Robert said.

That didn't sound good, James thought. Robert and Maggie Lehane must have cut all ties. He must remember that and not allude to them being in contact. Keep your mouth shut, James warned himself.

"So, you're not still living here, sir?" James said, treading carefully.

"I couldn't stick this place anymore, so I got the opportunity to spread my wings. No, that's a lie."

"Let's apply a need to know basis," James said.

"Thanks, James." Robert nodded gratefully.

James knew exactly what Robert had been getting up to since he last worked with him on the Joubert murders. His uncle, who was now the ex-superintendent of the local Garda station, had run off with the lovely Maria, the live-in help, to give her, as Katie often said, her full title. They had set up home together in another town, and for once James admired his uncle for having the gumption to stand up to his domineering wife Helen, the queen of snob-land.

Despite all this, James's uncle was very much in the know, and he still had a lot of influence with the long arm of the law. He had filled James in on Robert's whereabouts, and what he was doing at the present time.

Apparently, six months after Maggie went off on her new adventure, Robert rented out his house and moved away from Magnerstown. He got office work with the force in Waterford. He was inputting information and data, which he only did part-time because, with the rent he was getting for his house in Magnerstown, he could afford to pay for his new rental accommodation and not have to dip into his small earnings.

What else could he do, anyway? He was not the sort of man who would want to be learning new skills, and with his grumpy and stubborn attitude, he wouldn't last a day in an upskilling course. He would make too many enemies and be flung out on his ear.

'I wanted you to investigate the case, but I had to recommend Robert Carroll to work alongside you, seeing he is supposedly qualified in that field and you are not, but that's debatable.' James's uncle was laughing when he said that.

"So, here we are, back in Magnerstown," James said with a smile.

"Are you still studying law, James, in the capital city?"

"Yes, I am indeed, sir. Only because I'd be good for nothing else. If you are wondering why I got assigned to work with you…"

"Your uncle arranged it," Robert said, cutting in.

"That's right. Like us, he moved away too, but he still has influence here," James admitted.

"Good for him on both counts," Robert replied.

"So, what's on the agenda today?" James asked.

"Another pot of coffee first, don't you think? Tea for you, and then we show our faces over at the Garda station."

"It's been closed down, they moved to a smaller building farther up the road," James said.

"Is it a newer building?" Robert asked.

"Older," James replied.

"I don't like the sound of that," Robert said.

"I'll nip upstairs and change into my suit. I may as well look important, even if I'm not," James said.

"I haven't brought a suit with me. I never felt comfortable in one, to be honest. I always felt like a scarecrow when I wore one," Robert said. "I'll stick with my civvies if you don't mind."

James stood up and said, "I'll be as quick as I can."

"Take your time, James. Would you find someone and ask them to bring me…"

"To bring you a pot of coffee," James said, cutting in.

11

"And another batch of toast wouldn't go amiss. I don't know what it is about the country air, but it always gives me an appetite."

"Know exactly what you mean, sir." James laughed.

"Do you really?" Robert asked.

CHAPTER 3

"Would you mind showing us to the incident room?" James asked.

The desk sergeant tried not to laugh, but failed miserably.

This place is an even bigger kip than the old station, Robert mused as he and James followed the desk sergeant down a very long narrow corridor. You wouldn't want to be claustrophobic, he thought.

The smell of must and stale cigarette smoke hit the air as the door was thrown open by the laughing policeman.

"How many of you work here?" Robert asked.

"Just me and Celine. Cutbacks, you see."

"Celine, a Garda, is she?"

"No, she does the paperwork; not that there's much of that to be done, and you could write it on the back of an envelope. The only crime being committed here now is a bit of window breaking on a Saturday night."

"You weren't around two years ago when myself and my able-bodied assistant here, the one and only James Sayder, investigated the Joubert murders," Robert said.

"I'm a replacement, sir."

"Retired, did he? The old desk sergeant."

"He sure did. He is getting his pension from the man above."

"What are you talking about?" Robert asked.

"He died."

"So, where's Celine today then? On a one week on and one week off basis, is she? Seeing she has nothing to do but write on the back of envelopes?" Robert asked.

"She's gone on a tanning session to Spain, but she'll be back in a fortnight. By the way, she uses this room to have the odd sneaky ciggie, I can see your nose has detected that, you being a detective and all."

"Right, you can get back to your duties, we will take it from here," Robert said.

"There was a superintendent here named Sayder, are you a relation?" The desk sergeant looked directly at James.

"My uncle," James replied.

"I got a transfer here, the wife was born and bred in this town, she always wanted to come back. So, when the opportunity arose, I jumped at the chance," the desk sergeant explained.

Robert scowled at him.

Taking the hint, the man beat a hasty retreat.

James surveyed the room. There was a blackboard which was not terribly big, but the walls were wood panelled, so at least you could put some sticky notes up without doing damage. There was a wooden box containing several sticks of coloured chalk. He rooted through it, and right at the bottom he found a sole stick of white. There could be enough in that, he smiled wryly.

"Open the bloody window, will you, before I suffocate. Couldn't that Celine one go outside to smoke?" Robert coughed.

"Are you going to ring the coroner?" James asked.

As if on cue, Doctor Morris manoeuvred his large burly figure in through the open door.

"It stinks in here, and I am used to stinks, but this is what I'd call the king of stinks," Doctor Morris said, laughing.

Robert shook the doctor's outstretched hand. "We meet again," he said.

"Death is reuniting us," Doctor Morris replied.

Robert jerked a finger in James's direction. "I was about to ring you, as per my assistant's instructions."

"Hello, young Mr Sayder!" Doctor Morris boomed. "And tell me this, how's your uncle these days?"

"He is retired, but still married to the force."

Doctor Morris got down to business and said, "We have two bodies."

"Which were moved before we arrived, and if you don't mind me saying so, it was completely out of order," Robert added, snarling.

Doctor Morris ignored the sly dig and continued with his report. "I have identified one," he said.

"One?"

"Well, one of the two. A prayer book wrapped in plastic, which preserved it, was…"

"I take it there was a name on it," Robert interrupted.

"Pat Dillon was the name written on it."

"That's no proof really, is it? Might not have even been his," Robert said.

"Now, are you suggesting he stole it or something?" Doctor Morris said, laughing. "You'd want to be really mean to steal a holy thing. Although, now that I think of it, the church was broken into last week. They made off with the poor box. Now, if ever there was a low act, that was the lowest of the low."

"Is Father Scully still around?" James asked.

"The poor fellow ended up in a home for the bewildered, and then just gave up and died."

"He loved the old black and white movies, *The Devil at Four* was his favourite – Frank Sinatra and Spencer Tracy," James said.

"Sorry to have to interrupt your reminiscences, but could we get on with the case in hand?" Robert said with a growl.

"Sorry, sir," James said.

"One lad maybe fell in, and then the other tried to rescue him, or maybe not," Doctor Morris mused.

"You can leave the detection work to us," Robert said sharply.

"I'll be off. You have my number, for anything other than detection." Doctor Morris deliberately put emphasis on the word 'detection'.

"Send the desk sergeant down here, Doctor, on your way out. At least he will have local knowledge, and that is exactly what we need," Robert said.

The desk sergeant smiled when he was told the name of one of the victims.

"Know him, do you?" Robert guessed.

"There's two of them, Pat and Dick. A right gruesome twosome. Though, the Dick fellow was the ringleader, in my humble opinion."

"Into petty crime, were they?" Robert asked.

"Not quite, although... Actually, I will tell you another time. Mostly they were a proper pair of bullies, taunting poor misfortunes, and they did their fair share of fighting on a Saturday night after a feed of drink. And then that was followed by a feed of chips, which they duly threw up on the pavement. Wouldn't you pity the poor sod who had to clean it up from outside their front door?"

"Normal enough fellows so," Robert said, laughing.

"I'll give you the address of their mother, Mrs Dillon."

"We had better go and see her, James, before word gets out."

"I would highly recommend it, bad news travels fast in this town," the desk sergeant said.

"No change there then," Robert said.

"Indeed, news travels faster in Magnerstown than e-mail," the desk sergeant said, laughing.

"Broadband still giving trouble in town," James quipped.

"Come on for fuck sake, let's get out of here! I need a mug of coffee to resuscitate me," Robert said.

"I can make you one," the desk sergeant offered.

"I meant a decent mug of coffee, not brown fucking water," Robert said between gritted teeth.

"You are into your barista big time, are you?" The desk sergeant grinned.

James couldn't help but admire this man. He was approaching retiring age, but he was really up to date. He hated the concept that people over a certain age knew nothing about modern technology.

They knew everything there was to know about life, and the horrible thing was, just as they had gained all that vast experience, they did a disappearing act.

CHAPTER 4

"Are you Mrs Dillon?" James asked.

The woman looked so frail that James couldn't help feeling sorry for her. She was about to hear some tragic news, and she looked as if she could do without that kind of thing being foisted on her.

"We would like to have a word," Robert said.

It fell on James to make the introductions. "This is Detective Inspector Robert Carroll, and I am his assistant, James Sayder," he said.

Nellie Dillon offered to make a pot of tea as soon as they were seated at her kitchen table.

Robert declined the offer and placed his briefcase on the table. James would have liked a cup, but thought better of it when he caught Robert's steely eye.

"Please sit down, Mrs Dillon, I need to show you something," Robert said.

Nellie sat down on the edge of the chair looking extremely nervous.

Robert donned a pair of plastic gloves and then removed the prayer book from the briefcase. He opened it and showed Mrs Dillon the name written on the inside cover.

Robert noted the look on Mrs Dillon's face, which confirmed it was in fact the property of her son Pat.

"Can you tell us when he went missing?" Robert began.

"Just under a year ago now."

"Did you report it?"

"No, because…"

"Take your time. Would you like a drink of water?" Robert asked.

On cue, James went to the sink. There was a glass on the drainer which he half filled with water in case the poor woman dropped it.

Nellie's hand was visibly shaking as she took a sip. "I really hate that old council pop," she said.

"I don't blame you, Mrs Dillon. It's full of lime, and judging by the state of kettles, I shudder to think what our insides must look like," James said.

"So, what have they done over in England? The English police won't put up with what the crowd put up with here, and quite right too," Nellie Dillon stated.

"I am not following you," Robert said.

"The two of them scampered off to England, and to tell you the truth, I was glad they did. Well, to be honest, I missed Pat. He wasn't a bad lad, he wanted to be a priest, you know."

"Did you say England?" Robert asked.

"Yes, England, because they wouldn't last five minutes in America."

"Right, we are going to have to clarify this, Mrs Dillon. Do you know for certain they went to England?" Robert asked.

"I came home from work, I do for Miss Kneeshaw."

"Do?"

"I do cleaning for her. Only a few hours every second day. She's very generous, I'll give her that."

"Right, go on, Mrs Dillon. You came home from work…" Robert prompted.

"I got the pork chops onto the frying pan and called upstairs for the lads to come down. They always got up late on a Saturday. When they didn't come down, I went up to see what was wrong."

"They weren't there," Robert guessed.

"That's right, they weren't."

"And then?"

"I noticed their beds were still made up. Then I remembered they hadn't come home by the time I had gone to bed on the Friday night. So I presumed they'd got up to some shenanigans. I thought maybe they'd gone off for the weekend to some festival. They were devils for drinking and girling."

"You presumed."

"Yes, I presumed."

"I said nothing to nobody. But a few days later, their boss Mr Kelly called to see me. There's two of them, Bob and Jack. One of them is thin and the other is fat. I'll give you a fiver if you guess which one called."

"So, where's this place of work then?" Robert asked, ignoring the wager.

"Kelly's Cider Bottling Company."

"I know the place; it's in Grattan Street, sir," James said.

"So, what had this boss man to say about the boys?" Robert asked.

"He wondered where they were, thought they were sick, he said. I told him they were missing and he said I should report it," Nellie replied.

"But you didn't report it, did you?" Robert said.

"No, because Mr Kelly told me they'd been bawling off money. The odd few bob here and there. So then I was certain they'd been saving up to go to England. Dick was always saying he would love to get out of this town." Nellie paused to catch her breath and then continued, "Spread his wings and fly away, he used to say. Fat chance of that, I used to think. Like a homing pigeon, he'd be back within the day."

"Mrs Dillon, I am terribly afraid to say this, but we could have bad news for you," Robert said.

"He's dead, isn't he? Pat's dead. That's his prayer book. He always kept it in his pocket. If he had become a priest, he would be still alive," Nellie said as she fished a handkerchief out of her cardigan pocket and dried her eyes.

Robert waited for Nellie Dillon to compose herself before asking his next question. "Your other son Dick, tell us more about him," he said.

"Pure wild that one. Taken after his father for the boozing. His father drowned in a stream, you know. He was coming home drunk as a lord and wandered out of town. Fell into a stream, he did, and that was the end of him."

"Sorry for your loss," Robert said.

"You might think I'm cruel when I say this, but he was no loss. He was worth more dead than alive, widow's pension, if you get my meaning." Nellie winked.

"But the pension can't have been enough, seeing you had to do for Miss Kneeshaw," Robert said.

"Both of them are dead, aren't they? Pat and Dick are dead."

"From what we've got so far, yes, it seems likely," Robert replied.

"Is there anyone you want us to call? Anyone who could come and stay with you?" James asked.

"I'll be fine, thanks," Nellie replied.

"Are you sure of that? You've had an awful shock," James insisted.

"I'll be fine, don't worry," Nellie said with a smile.

* * *

Nellie Dillon let herself in through the side door with the key Miss Kneeshaw had entrusted to her. She was

21

proud of that. She had never told the boys about the key because she didn't trust them. They'd use it to rob the place. They were good at robbing, she knew that, because one time she'd found a crate of cider in the shed at the bottom of their garden when she went out there looking for a screwdriver. The door handle on her bathroom door had come loose, and she thought she'd try and fix it herself. It was still loose but it didn't matter now, she was quite safe because there was no danger of the lads bursting in on her when she was on the toilet.

Her purse was safe too; before, she'd have to hide it to stop money going missing. She knew Dick was the thieving little culprit. Just like his father, he was. Like father like son, as the saying goes.

Nellie forced herself to focus on the present. Today was cooker cleaning day, which was a bit of an overstatement. Miss Kneeshaw rarely used the cooker. The grill she did use, for toasting a few slices of bread, and the hob for boiling an egg or heating a few beans. The poor woman hardly ate at all, but she did like chocolate biscuits and buns, and endless pots of tea. When all was said and done, she was still hale and hearty for someone who was born during the war, and that could only mean there was nothing at all wrong with her diet.

Next on the agenda was the bedroom furniture. She loved lashing on the polish, with the lovely smell of lavender filling the air. Miss Kneeshaw had offered her a tin of the magic wax to take home, but she'd declined. There was nothing worth polishing at home.

Her first home after getting married was a flat over a furniture shop in Church Street. It was awful having to share the kitchen and bathroom with the other dwellers. The kitchen wasn't too bad because they'd worked out a rota for the use of it, but the bathroom was a different story. If you were bursting for the toilet, as often as not someone would be in it. Whereas she could hold it, the boys often peed in their pants. Eight years they had endured being cooped up in that damp hole of a place, until the council finally gave them a house.

The boys did so love the freedom of their new home, and they really relished playing out in the back garden. She often shed tears of joy as she observed them playing cowboys and Indians from the kitchen window.

She couldn't afford to buy them guns and holsters and cowboy suits like all the other boys their age had, but they improvised.

'Right. No more daydreaming, Nellie Dillon,' she told her reflection in the dressing table mirror.

Once her chores were finished, she made her way towards the parlour.

"Miss Kneeshaw," she called out.

"I'm in here with my lover," Miss Kneeshaw replied.

Nellie Dillon entered the room with a big smile on her face. "Is it the usual one you have, or have you traded him in for a younger model? I believe that's all the fashion," she said, laughing.

The table was laid out as usual for their afternoon tea. China cups and saucers, with matching teapot, jug and sugar bowl beautifully decorated with delicate pink roses. Two side plates with doilies on them, and a large plate in the middle, sporting assorted biscuits, rounded off the display.

Miss Kneeshaw liked the finer things in life; an educated woman of genteel nature, that's what Nellie liked so much about her boss.

"So, any news?" Miss Kneeshaw asked as she poured the tea.

"Yes, I have some news," Nellie said.

"Bit of town gossip, is it?" Miss Kneeshaw smiled.

"You could say that. At least it will be the talk of the town as soon as it gets out," Nellie said.

"Don't keep me in suspense," Miss Kneeshaw said with a frown.

"They have found Pat and Dick," Nellie said.

Miss Kneeshaw put the teapot down and looked into Nellie's face.

"They have found them? Where?" she asked.

"Just outside town, would you believe," Nellie said.

"Oh."

"And I was thinking they had gone to England, but all along they were right here," Nellie said.

Miss Kneeshaw took a handkerchief from her pocket and twisted it round her fingers.

"Yes, they've found them. And guess what?" Nellie said.

"What?"

"They're dead."

CHAPTER 5

"Accident prone, the Dillons are. First the husband, and then the two sons. What do you make of it all, James?" Robert said.

James removed his coat and placed it on the back of the chair before seating himself opposite Robert. "Mrs Dillon didn't seem too put out when we told her the news about her two sons. Sorry if I'm sounding a bit hard-hearted, but that's the impression I got, sir."

"She seemed relieved if anything, James."

"She is so delicate looking. Skin and bone, she is. You know what, though, I think she will get stronger now that she knows those two pests will not be coming back to pressurise her again. Although she seemed to have a bit of a soft spot for Pat, the failed priest," James said.

"You want a drink, James?" Robert asked.

"I'll get them. The usual for you, sir?" James offered.

"Yes, but I can't expect a college guy to lash out so. Put it on my tab, and whatever you are having yourself."

James returned ten minutes later with a brandy for Robert and an orange squash for himself.

"I thought you'd be a lager man," Robert remarked.

"I don't drink, sir."

"That's right, I'd forgotten that. Still no bad habits, eh?"

"We've all got our own little quirks," James said, and laughed.

"Met someone at the bar, did you? I was going to send out a search party," Robert said with a smile.

"I was talking to Mary."

"Mary?"

"The woman who served me at the bar."

"Chatting her up, were you?"

"She says the whole town's talking about the Dillon brothers. Speculation is running rife, apparently, and there's this." James pulled a copy of *The Crier* out of his coat pocket and placed it on the table in front of Robert.

Robert stared at the headline – *Ding Dong Bell, Pussy's in the Well.*

"Here we go again. I can't even be bothered to read it. So, if you wouldn't mind, tell me what it's about, James."

"It's just a load of drivel about the 'brothers grim'. Where they worked and all that malarkey. The tragic death of their father was mentioned too. The final sentence is interesting, though," James said.

"Who put them in, was it little Johnny Thin? Is that the best they can do, quote a nursery rhyme?" Robert said.

"Probably googled it."

Robert threw the paper back onto the table. "Get rid of that only-fit-for-fodder rubbish," he said.

James folded the paper and put it back into his coat pocket.

"Do you want to hear the information I gleaned from Mary, who is, by the way, filling in for the receptionist and the official barman tonight?" James asked.

Robert took a huge gulp of brandy and immediately regretted not having ordered a large one. There was only enough to wet the bottom of the glass to start with.

"Well, here's the deal," James began.

"Would you mind getting me another drink?" Robert asked.

James ordered a double this time, from the double jobbing Mary.

"I've put a little extra drop in." She winked.

Robert had drained the remains of drink number one when James returned with drink number two, which was possibly drink number three and more than likely drink number four all rolled into one, if Mary's wink was anything to go by.

"Right, James, do tell," Robert said. He had gravitated into a more relaxed state, and felt he could tolerate anything now that he was feeling nicely anaesthetised.

"It seems Dick Dillon got some young one up the duff. She was carted off to a mother and baby home by her uncle."

"I thought those places didn't exist anymore."

"Mary will get me the address she said, if the uncle isn't forthcoming."

"This Mary has many talents."

"As you say, sir, nothing like local knowledge," James said.

"Was she carted off before or after the daddy ended up in the well? Did you think to ask the lovely Mary that?" Robert asked.

"I did, sir, and yes, it was after he disappeared, apparently, that the flight into Egypt happened. I would imagine that when it became clear there was no chance of a shotgun wedding on account of the potential bridegroom having gone missing, extreme desperate measures had to be taken," James replied.

"You mean desperate as in making the problem disappear. In other words, sending the unfortunate girl out of sight and out of mind?" Robert asked.

"The final solution." James laughed, before adding, "Sorry, sir, that was a bit insensitive."

Robert fished his notebook out of his pocket and started jotting something down. He looked at his spider scrawl and realized he would have to take himself up to his room as soon as possible. He hadn't eaten since the morning and the brandy was starting to take effect big time. He would humour James for a few more minutes though, then drink up and excuse himself before he made a right eejit out of himself.

"Motive there, wouldn't you say, sir?"

"You didn't glean the uncle's name by any chance, did you?"

"Billy Barry is the man's name, and he lives at number five, Rosanna Road. And the girl's name, by the way, is Brigit."

"Billy Barry: a man with a motive," Robert said.

"But would you not think he would try and persuade the culprit to marry the girl though, rather than resort to killing him?" James remarked. "Wouldn't Mr Dick Dillon be worth more alive than dead?"

"Wanted dead or alive," Robert said, and laughed.

"It doesn't sit well with me," James said.

"Or else, to turn your theory the other way round, James, what if Uncle Billy didn't want a waster taking up with his precious niece. So, the only way to go was to take him out?" Robert said.

"But why would he kill the brother as well, sir? Unless, of course, the poor bugger tried to protect his kith and kin?" James reasoned.

"I should send you to get the drinks from now on," Robert said, and laughed. "We'll have the case solved in no time."

James remained silent as Robert drained his glass.

"Right, I'm off to my lonely bed in my lonely room," Robert said, adding, "I'm sure someone's written a song about all the lonely people in their lonely rooms."

James watched as Robert walked away unsteadily. He would wait ten minutes before making his way up to his own room, by which time Robert would probably be lying in his bed wrestling with his demons. The night before, he had heard him cry out whatever it was that was going on in his head. He was a tormented soul and he really did feel sorry for him. Where the hell was Maggie Lehane? James wondered. She at least had a calming effect on him.

If he had her telephone number, he would ring her right now and give her short shrift. No, he would do no such thing, he knew, but it felt good thinking about performing such a brave act.

CHAPTER 6

"Do you have a few moments to spare, Mr Barry?" Robert asked.

Billy made to close the door in Robert's face. "Listen, mate, I was born with one religion and I'm not interested in taking on a second one," he said.

"Sir, he thinks we're trying to convert him to..." James said.

"I know," Robert cut in.

"Why don't you try next door, she's game for anything, that one. Just tell her you'll pay all her bills for her and she'll sign up immediately," Billy said with a sneer.

Robert put his foot in the door and said, "We are investigating the death of a young man who is known to your niece. So, if you don't mind, a bit of cooperation wouldn't go astray, Mr Barry."

"You're talking about the Dillon fucker, aren't you? Good riddance to him, as far as I am concerned."

"So, you know what's happened to him," Robert said.

"Me and the whole town are in receipt of that information. Good news travels fast in this place, you know."

"Good news?"

"Alright, ye best come in. I want to hear all the gory details."

Billy led them to the kitchen. It was old-fashioned but clean, Robert noted as he looked around before plonking himself down onto the chair Billy was pointing to. James, on instruction, sat on the chair beside Robert.

Billy made his way to the worktop where a gleaming silver kettle stood in all its glory. He pressed the on switch and, facing his guests, he said, "Like my new kettle, lads? I decided to splash out, those cheap ones don't last pissing time."

"No tea for us, but if you want one yourself, do feel free to go ahead and make some," Robert said.

Billy switched the kettle off and sat down opposite Robert and James.

"So, is it true what everyone is saying? Dickie bird and his sidekick, Pat a cake, were murdered?" Billy asked.

"It's not confirmed yet," Robert said.

"They could have been out there drunk, horsing around. Their father met an untimely death while drunk," Billy said.

"So we were informed, by those who feel it's their business to inform," Robert replied.

"They were murdered. Go on, admit it, or you wouldn't be here asking questions, would you?" Billy said.

"We understand your niece has had a baby," Robert said.

"The good for nothing fucker interfered with her," Billy said peevishly.

"We might like to talk to her," Robert said.

"She's down the country in a retreat place until she gets on her feet. The whole thing took a lot out of her, she's a delicate girl."

"Were you angry with Dick Dillon? I could really understand if you wanted to give him a good hiding."

"He wouldn't be worth doing time for. But I do hope he suffered before he died, him and his pansy brother.

You don't know the half of it," Billy said, as he tried to put on a brave face.

How much did these two know? he wondered. When Brigit told him she was in the family way, he had freaked out. History repeating itself, he realized. Brigit's mother, his sister, had got herself pregnant too, and the guy who did the dirty deed put it all over town that she was easy. The 'town bike' was the term he'd used to describe her. It all came to a head one night in the Criterion Pub.

The smarmy fucker was a little bit under the weather, and when he spotted Billy sitting in the corner minding his own business, he just couldn't resist having a go. Up he staggered to where Billy was sitting and said, sneering into his face, "Billy lad, you should send that sister of yours out to make a living with what she's got under her skirt. No, on the other hand, she wouldn't make much, they'd be asking for a credit note."

Billy saw red. He was sick of the rumours that were circulating around town. He didn't exactly remember every detail of what happened in the pub that night because he was blind with rage. He did remember punching the smarmy git in the face and him falling backwards onto a table of glasses behind him. He was a snivelling wimp after all, because only a wimp would manage to die of a heart attack.

Judge Mangan had sentenced Billy to five years in prison for manslaughter. It was so unfair, but then the old goat got his comeuppance when he was killed by that South African fellow, Greg Joubert, two years ago.

Billy felt karma had kicked in, and the five years he'd done in prison all those years ago were worth it, after all.

Billy studied the two detectives, Punch and Judy they reminded him of. According to the local talk, the older one, Carroll, wasn't worth a fuck. But the young one was clever. He was the one who'd solved those murders two years ago. Carroll, on the other hand, couldn't solve a children's crossword puzzle.

"You might give us your niece's whereabouts, just in case we want to ask her a few questions," Robert said.

"What can she tell you?" Billy asked.

"She may know the enemies Dick had, that sort of thing."

"Everyone in town hated him, especially that young girl with the calliper. They were always bullying her, calling her names."

"Are you talking about the McGrath girl?" James asked.

"Yes, I am. Marie McGrath got polio when she was small. Her mam and dad run the chipper on the main street."

Robert beckoned to James to jot down the information.

"Although they might not be running the place for much longer, from what I hear," Billy said.

"Why's that then, selling up, are they? Moving away to start a new life, or whatever it is people move away for nowadays?" Robert asked.

"There's a rumour going around that their chipper and the jewellers are going to be closed down. The houses in the middle are already condemned, so that just leaves the shops," Billy replied.

"So, what happened to the owners of the houses in the middle? I'm sure you won't mind filling us in, Billy," Robert said.

"That poor fellow Mossie Harrington had to leave his home, and he had been living there all his life."

"We must follow that up. Jot it down, James."

Billy knew the best thing to do was to get the limelight off himself and talk about everyone and anything, just to distract these two foragers. "Imagine condemning those houses. They were solidly built, not like the cardboard excuses they are churning out nowadays. No, as far as I am concerned, that's a bloody stroke if ever there was one," he said.

"Ulterior motives is your reckoning, Billy; so, who would be in the frame for pulling that kind of a stunt?" Robert asked.

Billy didn't like where the conversation was going, so he immediately changed the subject. "Here's Brigit's address, but I would really prefer if you didn't have to talk to her. She's very vulnerable at the moment. She had a very difficult birth, you know, and she's not herself at all," he said.

"We will tell you if we have to see her. And if we do, maybe you might like to come with us," Robert suggested.

Billy rose to his feet. He was relieved the interview had come to an end without having it pointed out to him by the two bloodhounds that he'd done time. He could just imagine the meal they would make out of that. "I'll see you out, shall I?" he said.

"Thanks, and we will be in touch if the need arises," Robert said.

"I take it Brigit's mother is no longer with us." James made the observation as they reached the front door.

"She died two years ago. It was cancer that got her," Billy replied.

"Sorry to hear that," James said.

"Nice meeting you both," Billy said.

"He couldn't wait to get rid of us," James remarked in response to the slamming of the door after they had stepped out onto the street.

"He looked shifty alright," Robert said.

"What do you think, sir?" James asked as they made their way back to Dobbyn's Hotel.

"I think he would have liked to have killed Dick Dillon, but then he didn't have to, because someone else did it for him. There's a possibility he might know more than he is letting on, though."

"As you say, sir, everyone is a suspect at this stage."

"Do I say that? I sound like one of those fictitious detectives on the telly. Not that I watch them, of course."

James laughed.

"Look into the condemning of the houses and shops on the street, James."

"It would be the council, would it not, who would have the power to do that?" James asked.

"You would imagine so, but do a bit of digging, James. You never know what might come to the surface," Robert said.

"I've been digging all my life and I nearly got to hell, my uncle dug potatoes and he struck an oil well," James said, and laughed.

"What?"

"It's a song, sir," James explained.

CHAPTER 7

James laid his purchases down on the counter and smiled at the pretty young woman as she checked them out.

"So, tell me this and tell me no more: are you having a party tonight as well?" she asked.

"As well as who?"

"You're staying in Dobbyn's Hotel, aren't you?"

"I am, indeed," James said with a grin. "And what else have you heard about me?"

"That boss of yours is a right grumpy old so-and-so, isn't he?"

"You must have inside information."

"I have, as it happens: one of the girls working in the hotel is a friend of my brother Gerry. Platonic, I hasten to add. Everything to do with Gerry is platonic."

James laughed. Everyone knew everyone, and everybody knew everything about everybody in Magnerstown. They probably knew who killed the Dillon brothers too, but were naturally not going to furnish that information.

"He was in here earlier on, buying a bottle of brandy," she said.

"Your brother?"

"No, silly. Your boss. And yes, my inside information was correct. He was rude to me, and he didn't even say 'thank you'. But then, of course, he probably thought he was doing me a favour keeping me in a job with his purchase," she said.

"Yes, I should have picked up on the clue, brandy is a favourite of his alright. Should I be confirming my boss's secrets, though?" James said, and laughed.

"I think he is a bit paranoid too, because, out of the blue, he said 'isn't a fellow entitled to have a drink on his birthday?'" she said.

"He is going to have a private party with just the one guest: himself," James said.

"Speaking of parties, Mrs Dillon has been partying ever since those wasters of sons of hers went missing. She comes in here to get a few things on tick. Tick means getting stuff on credit, just in case you don't know on account of you being a city boy and all that jazz."

"Believe it or not, I do know what tick means. But I didn't think shops offered that service anymore," James said.

"Every penny counts in a small business like this, and another thing we have to do is to stay open when the Centro Supermarket is closed for the night. That's when the money is to be made."

"That Centro place is so small, I am surprised they have the tenacity to call themselves a supermarket," James said.

"It's bigger than this shop, isn't it? Twice the size, so I suppose they could give themselves the supermarket title."

"Did Mrs Dillon ever talk about her sons to you; after they went missing, that is?" James asked. He could see this young woman was in the mood for talking and why not find out what he could by offering a listening ear.

"In the beginning, Mrs Dillon used to say it was great that she could come and go as she pleased. She could eat whatever she wanted to eat, and if she didn't feel like cooking, no one was going to give off to her about it. She was a free agent, she used to say with a big smile on her face."

"Did they come in here, her two sons?"

"Tell me about it. Dick was always getting cigarettes and asking for them to be charged up to his mother's account. Cheeky devil. Always saying something smart. No wonder he got himself killed."

"Be careful what you say, it could get you killed," James said.

"That's a good one, I must write that down in my little notebook. I write short stories and I am always looking for ideas. They say that many a book was written thanks to an overheard conversation. Not that I'll ever graduate to a book. I am exaggerating when I say I write short stories: two thousand words is the most I've ever managed. I have submitted a lot of my stuff to several competitions, but I did get longlisted one time," she said proudly.

"There's plenty of material in this town, I am sure," James said.

"Yes, a murder most foul we had two years ago. In fact, three murders all in one go."

"Yes, that's right; I was involved in the investigation, but you weren't here then, were you?" James asked.

"I came back from England last year because the girl who worked here left to get married. The guy she married is loaded, so she don't have to work no more. Some people are so jammy, would you not agree?"

"You saw the job advertised, did you?" James asked.

"Well, to be honest, my grandfather owns this place and he offered me the job. England, I am afraid, had lost its lustre, so I jumped at the chance. I didn't admit the real reason I took him up on his offer, naturally. I kind of made out I was doing him a favour by coming back. And you know what, that's true to a certain extent. I am, as it happens, doing him a huge favour, because nobody else in their right mind would put up with the unsociable hours."

"Open all hours, eh?" James said, and laughed.

"I don't half jabber a lot, no wonder my mouth goes dry," she explained as she opened a bottle of water and took a large gulp.

"Getting back to the Dillon brothers, not very popular, were they, by all accounts?" James prompted.

"The amount of people they rubbed up the wrong way was absolutely unbelievable."

"So, they had several arch enemies?"

"That poor girl in the chipper was tormented by them. She must have been delighted when they disappeared off the face of the earth."

"Did everyone assume they'd done a runner?"

"It was common knowledge that Dick got Brigit Barry into trouble. The foregone conclusion was he'd gone off to England to escape a shotgun wedding. Of course, he had to take his gimpy brother with him because them two were like conjoined twins," she said.

"So, how much do I owe you?" James asked.

"Five euro and ten cents. Ah, go on with you, the fiver will do," she said.

James paid for his bag of goods and headed for the door. "You might come for a drink sometime," he called over his shoulder. He didn't want her to see the embarrassment on his face when she made up some excuse not to take him up on his offer.

"My name's Lilly, by the way, and yes, I'd love to go for a drink with you," she called after him.

CHAPTER 8

Robert couldn't wait to open the bottle of brandy he had bought from that cheeky little one in the huckster shop, the way she was looking at him, like he was the beast from the east.

He would just have the one drink in peace, without James looking at him like he was an alcoholic or something. Non-drinkers didn't seem to understand the escapism alcohol offered. A liquid chill pill.

Robert placed his little radio-cum-CD player on the locker by the bed and plugged it in. He had wrapped shirts and jumpers around it for protection when he packed it into his suitcase.

Today was his birthday, and nobody knew, except for himself of course, and his mother and his father if they were still alive. No, he was not going to dwell on all that emotional shit tonight. He would just have a drink to mark the special occasion. Special occasion, what a joke that was.

The CD was already in the player, so he pressed the button for the 'repeat automatically' function. That was one great feature, hats off to the fellows who designed it for lazy fuck-faces like him.

He sat down on the comfortable armchair beside a table by the window. This is the life, he thought as he poured out a large measure and laid back with glass in hand listening to Satie, his favourite composer.

He knew he was going to fail miserably with the promise he had made not to focus on himself tonight of all nights. His thoughts started to race, and he wanted them to stop, but he knew he had boarded the roller coaster of failure, misery and regret.

Take the fairer sex for starters, his experience with them was a total disaster and he had no problem admitting it, if only to himself.

First, there was the lovely Annie whom he met while working in France, and he had her to thank for introducing him to all things French. It was she who had persuaded him to settle back in Magnerstown, and he duly agreed. She had a job at Cliff's Restaurant and all was going well until he caught her and Cliff in a compromising position. Annie had sworn Cliff was harassing her and he hadn't believed her. But he should have, because she was telling the truth, as he later found out. To be perfectly honest, he wanted to believe she was having an affair with Cliff because the relationship on his part had gone stale. He just wanted out and the opportunity manifested itself.

Maggie Lehane, editor of the local rag, came on the scene when he was investigating the Joubert murders. They muddled along well together, then she upped and left for a wonderful opportunity in London which she couldn't turn down. She dumped him, simple as that. Don't even go there, he warned himself, and drained and refilled the glass right up to the top this time. So much for one drink; one is never enough with you, he rebuked himself.

The sound of loud knocking on the door brought him to his senses. Looking at his watch, he realized he had dozed off for two whole hours.

"Hold your horses," he shouted above the music.

He opened the door and found a nervous young woman standing outside. She couldn't be more than sixteen, he realized.

"I just want to ask you something," she whispered.

"Come in," he said. Then he wondered if it was a wise thing to do.

"Thanks, I won't delay you. My name is Marie McGrath, by the way."

Robert turned off the CD player.

"That's a French composer you are listening to. Gnossienne; Satie, isn't it?" Marie said.

"Yes, that's right."

"When he died, they found seven grey suits in his wardrobe. I know all about him," Marie smiled.

"Are you a fan?"

"I am learning all about the great composers in my English class."

"You have a good teacher, by the sounds of it."

"Miss Gohery. She's the best."

"And I'd say you're the best pupil in the class," Robert said, smiling.

"It wouldn't be hard for me, the rest of them are only interested in boys and make-up, and dresses up to their arses. Sorry, that's rude."

"It's the truth, I'd imagine, not taking away from you being the best in the class." Robert smiled.

"Is it true that the Dillons are dead?" Marie asked.

"It would seem so."

"Thank God for that. I won't have to worry no more now."

"Give you a hard time, did they?"

Marie pointed to her calliper. "Always calling me a freak, they were."

"Polio, is it? I thought that was eradicated a long time ago."

"I was born in Belgium, that's where I got it. There was an outbreak and I was unfortunate. Story of my life, really."

"Sorry to hear that," Robert said.

"My mother is from Belgium and my father is Irish. He was out there working in a beer factory when he met her. They came back to Magnerstown to take up the family business when my grandad died fourteen years ago."

"McGrath's chipper on the main street, I know it," Robert said.

"Do you?"

"I used to live here myself; well, on and off, really."

"Wait a minute, you were here on the case of the murders that South African fellow committed," Marie said.

"Me and my long-haired lover from Liverpool. Sorry, that's not true. He's not my lover, and he doesn't come from Liverpool."

"He's gorgeous, all the girls in my class are talking about him. Like a prince, he is," Marie said, gushing.

"Prince of darkness," Robert said with a laugh.

"Sorry?"

"Take no notice of me, I am inclined to make the strangest of remarks at times," Robert said with a grin.

"My father's the same. He is always saying funny things which only he understands," Marie said.

"So, you must be relieved now that your tormentors are no longer in the land of the living," Robert said.

"It might sound cruel, but yes, I am very relieved they have met their Waterloo." Marie laughed.

"Apart from the Dillons, does anyone else bother you about your condition?" Robert asked.

"No, it was just those Dillon bullies. Much as I criticise the girls in my class, they have never once made any derogatory remarks about me. So, maybe I shouldn't be so hard on them, maybe I shouldn't be going on about their little idiosyncrasies."

"Well, you need to worry no more about your tormentors, because they have, as you said so yourself, met their Waterloo."

Marie turned to go. "Right, I'll leave you to enjoy the rest of your night," she said.

Robert opened the door for her.

"You are quite nice," Marie said, smiling at him. "Not at all like what they are saying about you."

Robert laughed. He could well imagine the impression the townspeople had of him, but it didn't bother him one bit. He was here to do a job and the quicker he could get it over with, the quicker he could get back to normality, whatever that was.

* * *

Marie's thoughts were racing. The real reason she had come here tonight was to see if she could detect, which was funny really, seeing she wasn't a detective, but she just wanted to suss the man out. She just wanted to see if he suspected her father might have murdered the Dillon brothers. Her father certainly had a reason: protecting his daughter. That would be considered a motive.

This detective fellow would know she was always being bullied by them. She was a victim, everybody knew it, and they would be quick to point it out. That's people for you, wanting to be seen in a good light by the long arm of the law.

What could she say to find out if her father was in the fray? Nothing, that's what she would say, it would only draw attention to the matter. She knew her father had nothing to do with it, didn't she? Well, he didn't, did he?

* * *

Robert broke in on her thoughts and said, "If that's all then, I'll bid you goodnight."

"Thank you for letting me talk. I needed to know for sure they were gone. You do understand, don't you?" Marie asked.

"If anyone else is bothering you, please feel free to let me know and I will see that they are sorted out," Robert said.

Yes, there was someone else bothering her: her mother. But you couldn't say that, could you? And even if you did, she wouldn't be arrested, would she? Instead of disclosing this fact, Marie simply stated, "Thank you, but everything is fine now."

"Goodnight, safe home," Robert said, and closed the door.

He should have offered to walk her to her home, but he was in no fit state to do so. She'd be alright though, seeing those tormentors of hers were out of the way.

He was relieved to see there was still brandy in the bottle. He poured out the last of it and sat back down into the armchair. He laid back to savour the last few hours of his birthday. He hoped the young woman hadn't spotted the bottle. It wouldn't create a good impression. But then, what about it? A person was entitled to have a drink in the privacy of their hotel room, especially when they were far from home, he thought as he put the glass to his lips. Home, that was a good one. "Happy Birthday, Robert," he said, and laughed sarcastically. All he wanted now was total oblivion.

* * *

Marie thought about the lonely man in his room as she made her way back home. He was quite normal from what she could see, having a drink in the privacy of his own room. He was quite right, given the prices the hotel was charging. Her father was always going on about it, five euro for a tiny drop of spirits. Publicans had no conscience at all, he'd say.

She liked Robert Carroll, or Detective Inspector, or whatever you were supposed to call him. She really liked him for the sole reason that he seemed lost and lonely. He was just like herself, really. They had something in common, both lost and very lonely.

CHAPTER 9

Robert pointed to the blackboard, which hadn't seen much chalk. "So, what do we know already?" he asked.

James fished his notebook out of his pocket and started to leaf through it. There wasn't much to see, but he had to show willingness.

Robert answered his own question. "Feck all, is all we know, and at the rate we are going, we will be here for the rest of our lives."

The desk sergeant burst through the door without knocking.

"Morning," Robert said sarcastically.

"Just a bit of information," the desk sergeant began.

"Well?"

"Did you speak to the jeweller Miss Kneeshaw?"

"No, why?"

"The Dillon lads tried to break into her shop before they went missing," the desk sergeant revealed.

"So, they didn't succeed then? I take it the clue is in the word 'tried'," Robert said.

"It was the old boy next door to Miss Kneeshaw's shop who reported it. When Celine went to ask Miss

Kneeshaw if she wanted to press charges against them, she said she was going to do no such thing."

"Celine does a bit of Garda work too, does she? One of those real all-rounder types," Robert said, grinning.

The desk sergeant ignored the dig and went on to defend Celine in her absence. "An attempted break-in wasn't worth pursuing, so Celine was quite sensible about the matter and didn't push Miss Kneeshaw."

"Did you make a note of it?" James asked. "The time, date, and all that. Did you or Celine record this attempted break-in? They must have done damage to a door or a window. That could come in under the heading of criminal damage. She could have got compensation from them, instead of drawing on her insurance."

"The truth is, Mrs Dillon works for Miss Kneeshaw, so we presumed she didn't want to upset her employee by taking a case against her two sons," the desk sergeant explained.

"This old boy who reported the incident, we should go and see him. What's his name?" James asked.

"I'm afraid that's out of the question because the man died a few weeks after the incident, and cruel as it sounds, it was just as well for his own sake."

"Why is that?" James asked.

"He would have had nowhere to go, no relative to take him in, and it would have killed him if he ended up in Mary I's nursing home. He was an outdoors man, loved going for long walks, enjoyed the fresh air; confinement would have done him in, that's for sure."

Robert felt he had to make an input. "So, he lived in one of the houses that were condemned?"

"He did, right next door to Mossie Harrington."

"Ah yes, the lovely Maggie Lehane's new tenant," Robert said with a scowl.

James shot Robert a look. What had happened between those two? he wondered. Why had it ended before it had actually begun? Robert and Maggie, the modern version of Romeo and Juliet. Well, a more mature Romeo and Juliet to be correct. He tried to keep a straight face as the thought crossed his mind.

The bell on the front desk shrilled in the background.

"Duty calls." The sergeant retreated, banging the door on his way out.

"You wouldn't want to have a headache with him around," Robert said, cringing. He didn't reveal that he did have a headache, a real humdinger, thanks to the brandy he poured down his throat the night before.

"Maybe we should pay Miss Kneeshaw a visit," James suggested.

"Why? No crime's been committed, has it? Apart from your allegation of criminal damage to property."

"I know, but…"

"Come on, James, spit it out."

"If the houses in between Miss Kneeshaw's shop and the chipper have been condemned, is it possible the shops have too?"

"That whole street is an eyesore," Robert said. "Best thing for it is to demolish it all, build something useful there."

"But those buildings are beautiful, they are part of the heritage of this town, wouldn't you agree, sir?"

"Heritage, my arse," Robert scoffed.

"I also think…"

"Oh yeah, what is it now?" Robert said, interrupting.

James realized Robert had a hangover. He had let it slip to Lilly in the corner shop that it was his birthday when he'd bought a bottle of brandy to celebrate, and she'd told James. Maggie obviously hadn't been in touch to wish him a happy birthday, which would account for his foul mood this morning. The two of them should have their heads banged together to make them see sense.

What was he thinking? After all, he and Katie had drifted apart too: she had sent him loads of text messages when she first went to Australia, but they had tapered off

49

to one a week, then one a month, and now, nothing. She had obviously met somebody else and was sparing his feelings by not saying anything. The texts now were, 'Hi James, any news?' His replies were the usual, 'No news, all quiet here.' They were a right pair, Robert and himself, when it came to matters of the heart. Unlucky in love.

"Well, you also think?" Robert asked.

"You know what, sir? I have completely forgotten what I was going to say," James replied.

"Can't have been that important then, can it, if you've forgotten it already," Robert said.

"I'm starving, sir. The breakfast this morning wasn't much to write home about. Even the tea was cold, and you said your coffee was lukewarm," James said.

"Yes, remember lukewarm Benny in Dunworth's Pub, famous for his lukewarm coffee?" Robert said, and laughed.

"He's left, and I heard the new replacement is exactly the opposite, his coffee is so hot, it would melt the enamel off your teeth," James said.

"Would there be any chance he might come and work at Dobbyn's? Honestly, it's hit and miss in that excuse of a hotel. It all depends on who's on duty in the kitchen, I have noticed. The so-called chef is total crap, but the woman who fills in for him when he is off, is good. She probably gets a fraction of what he is getting, but she deserves to get more than him. Chef, my arse. He probably took a poxy six-week course and got a certificate at the end of it. Surely you can take online courses now. All you have to do is sign up and pay with your credit card, which I hasten to add, every Tom Dick and fucking Harry has now. You can get qualifications in almost anything, if you have the plastic dosh card. It's all…"

James waved his hand in the hope that the gesture would stop Robert's long-winded speech and said, "I think we would not only work much better, but feel much better if we had some decent hearty sustenance inside us."

"Are you thinking what I'm thinking?" Robert asked, brightening up.

"A slap-up brunch in Dunworth's Pub, would I be right in thinking that's what's on your mind, sir?" James said.

"Onwards, James, and don't spare the horses."

"Tally ho," James said, grinning.

CHAPTER 10

HOME OR HERE – the sign was written in bold capitals with a black marker, and James couldn't help smiling at the statement. Dining here would be a bit of a problem if there was a crowd. There were just two tables as far as he could make out, and one seemed to be occupied. He spotted the books, and a tub of ice cream with something that looked like a small protractor sticking out of it. His eyes rested on a familiar tin beside the books. Mathematical instruments, he noted, exactly like the ones he had during his schooldays. Things hadn't changed much. The tables were blue Formica with silver edgings and legs. They were, if he rightly remembered, very popular in the sixties.

James approached the counter.

"What would you like?"

He looked in the direction the voice had come from, but he couldn't see the questioner in the midst of the rising vapour. The plunging of a fresh basket of chips into the boiling dripping was the cause of all the steam, he guessed.

"It'll clear soon," the voice assured him.

"A bag of chips," James said. As an afterthought, he added, "Please." Must not forget his manners, especially where a lady was concerned.

"Here or take away?"

"Here."

He could just about make her out, young and pretty, and she was pointing an equally pretty finger in the direction of the vacant table.

"I'll bring them over. Two euro, please," she said.

After James handed over the coin, he did as he was bid and headed for the unoccupied table.

There were posters of bull fights all around the walls. Handsome matadors in brightly coloured garb holding red cloaks aloft featured in every one of them. Was that where the term red rag to a bull came from? How unusual, he thought, posters like those in a little place like this. Was it possible the owners were Spanish, or maybe they had a villa over there to retire to sunnier climes during the winter months? They must be well-off. This chipper business was probably only a sideline to keep them amused.

The jukebox in the corner caught his eye. The machine gleamed; the glass and chrome had been polished to within an inch of its life. Someone was doing a great job with the upkeep of it. It was obviously cherished by the owner, he concluded.

He didn't see her approach and only became aware of her presence when she landed the bag of chips on the table and touched his shoulder.

"I took the liberty of putting salt and vinegar on them. All the men seem to like loads of salt and vinegar," she said.

When he looked up, she had already seated herself at the other table. "Thanks for the liberty," James said.

"If you were taking them back to the hotel, I'd have put them into a second bag to keep them warm."

"The hotel," James echoed. She knew where he was staying. Well, that shouldn't surprise him: after all, the whole town knew.

Her blue eyes bore into his. "The customers' every need is met here. Just saying, in case you didn't know."

James pointed to the jukebox. "How much is it to play a record?" he asked.

"Two euro gets you two plays. You can insert two one-euro coins, or a two-euro one; you are spoilt for choice."

"Everything is two euro round here," James cajoled. "This is the land of the two euro."

She laughed at that and then started writing in the open copybook.

"English Essay," James said, guessing.

"My favourite subject, would you believe," she replied.

"Mine too. I mean, when I was at school, it was the thing I liked the best. Maths came second, I loved working things out. Still do. I see you've made use of your maths set in more ways than one."

When James noticed she was staring at the melted contents of the tub, he felt he had to apologize. "That's my fault for delaying you, can I buy you another one to make up for it?"

"Don't be silly, I was taking a liberty anyway."

"Treating yourself to an ice cream's a liberty, is it?"

"It always goes wrong when I do something I'm not supposed to do. It's like I'm being given a message that I'm not meant to enjoy anything at all."

"Are you sure you wouldn't like another one?" James asked. "I'd be delighted to treat you, if you'd let me."

"Eat your chips before they go cold, or else it'll be me who will be apologising for spoilt goods."

James opened the bag and started to tuck in. "These are absolutely delicious. You really know how to cook a chip," he said.

"We use dripping from the local butcher. Harry is his name. He claims his mother always used it to fry chips when he was growing up, and it was her who gave him the idea and the recipe for his award-winning dripping."

"A recipe for dripping, that sounds a bit far-fetched," James said, and laughed.

"I totally agree with you. What is it? Only grease rendered down from roast meat, surely," she said.

"I love the posters," James said, changing the subject.

"I don't. Killing defenceless animals is cruelty personified."

"I wouldn't say bulls are entirely defenceless, they would kill you given half a chance," James replied.

"Only if you taunted them."

"Is there a Spanish interest in the family?" James asked.

"Belgium is the foreign link. My mother comes from there. If you ever have the pleasure of meeting her, she will tell you what chips are called in her native country."

"Pommes frites," James said, smiling.

"An educated man. I like that, not many like you in this backward country town. But then, you're not from round here so, that says it all, really."

James made his way over to the corner to study the jukebox. "A working jukebox, what a treasure," he said.

"Everything works here, including myself. Only I work the most, if only it was admitted. You wouldn't believe the amount of chores I have to do here, and as for my homework, that's always on the back-burner."

"I'm James, by the way."

"Marie is my name."

James studied the playlist and fumbled in his pocket for a coin. He was in luck, he realized – he had a two-euro coin left. He inserted it and pressed the letter C and the number one.

The strains of "Got myself a crying, talking, sleeping, walking, living doll," filled the air. His mother was a big fan of Cliff Richards. She would have loved this if she were here, he knew.

When the song ended, James returned to the table and folded his chip bag closed. He'd eat the rest back in his room. Marie had given him a mountain load, he'd noticed, possibly because she thought he needed fattening up, like a turkey for the Christmas table.

"You've only played one, you can get two," Marie said.

"Would you like to choose one?" James asked.

"Don't mind if I do. Can you do it for me?" Marie replied.

"So, what's it to be?" James asked.

"Press the letter L and the number five," Marie replied.

Bobby Darin singing 'Dream Lover' started to play.

Marie closed her eyes and listened to every word, while James took the opportunity to gaze at her unobserved. She reminded him of the marble statue of Aphrodite, one of his favourites when he was going through his fascination with art stage.

"So, what's the story with the jukebox," James asked when the song ended.

"It belonged to my grandfather, my father's dad. He had it shipped over from England in the sixties. A man before his time, as they say. And as you can see, we are still stuck in the sixties. Nothing's changed here, we are in a time warp."

"To give her credit, I must say your mother does a good job keeping the jukebox looking like new," James remarked.

"You must be joking! Queen Hanne of Belgium would break a nail if she tackled that chore."

"Queen Hanne, the woman who will educate me in regard to pommes frites." James laughed.

"The very one." Marie laughed.

"So, who looks after the jukebox then?" James asked.

"My father, and you want to see him cleaning and buffing the silver parts and the glass. Bet you didn't see one fingerprint on it until you graced it with your own.

Tomorrow, he will be wiping them off. It will be like you never laid a finger on it."

"You can tell him I was most impressed," James said.

"He'll love you for that."

"Tell him I love the posters too."

"He brought them back from one of his trips up north. He likes them, so I have never actually told him how much I hate them. Sometimes you have to take other people's feelings into consideration, don't you."

"So, how did they meet, your parents?" James asked.

"He was in Belgium working in a beer factory and she was a wages clerk. And before you ask me what he was doing there, I don't think he even knows the answer to that himself."

"Sowing his wild oats, I presume," James said.

"Apparently, he did sow some oats, because there was a quick trip down the aisle. That much I have learned from listening at keyholes," Marie said, and laughed.

"Keyholes are great educators."

"They came back here when my grandad died. They took over the business, which was all Hanne's idea, by the way," Marie explained.

"So, is she having a night off, your mother, seeing she's not here?"

"She's having more than a night off," Marie said, and smiled knowingly.

James knew it was an innuendo, but he didn't want to pry.

"My father is upstairs. If I want him, all I have to do is holler."

"That's good."

"Did your boss tell you I called to see him?" Marie asked.

"No, he didn't," James said.

"I wanted to be sure those bullies got what was coming to them, so I had this mad rush to the head and went to see him. It was cheeky of me going to his room in the hotel, but he didn't seem to mind."

"Those Dillon fellows tormented you, didn't they?"

"The last thing that horrible Dick Dillon did to me was really low. He pulled my beret off my head and then he pushed it into the pillar box outside Kneeshaw's jewellers' shop."

"So, did you get it back in the post?" James asked, grinning. "Sorry, that was a bit insensitive." He bit his lip.

"Miss Kneeshaw saw it all going on. She sorted it out, though. She got the post office crowd to open the letterbox and retrieve it. And yes, you could say I got it back in the post," Marie said, and laughed.

"Those Dillons sound like a right pair of thugs who are absolutely no loss at all," James said.

"Their mother is a lovely woman, though. I hope she is enjoying her freedom now that they're gone for good."

"Did your father know about this aggro you were getting from those two yobs?" James ventured.

"What you really want to ask is, did my father ever take them to task?"

"Just wondered if he knew, that's all," James said.

"I didn't tell him the half of it because I was afraid if I did, he'd kill…" Marie stopped abruptly.

James picked up the chip bag. "I'll finish these back in my hotel room," he said.

"Will I wrap them up for you?" Marie asked.

"Not at all, they're grand," James answered.

"You'll have to make a run for it, you don't want them getting cold."

After James departed, Marie closed her copybook. She couldn't concentrate now, she realized. She'd have to finish her essay in the morning because her mind was on other things.

He was nice, this James fellow. Gorgeous, in fact. That long shiny hair of his was just divine. She loved his lovely soft voice. If ever she were to write a book, she would base her main character on him.

Did Edna O'Brien have a real Mr Gentleman in mind when she wrote *The Country Girls*, she wondered.

Tonight, in the privacy of her bed, she would go over every word this lovely James had said. He would be her very own Mr Gentleman, smiling at her from top to toe. Thank God he didn't see the calliper on her leg tonight. But how could she hide it from him in the future, because he would hate her from the minute he saw it.

CHAPTER 11

James had managed to muster up the courage to suggest to Robert that a thorough search of the Dillon brothers' rooms might be a good idea. He had been careful to put it in such a way as to make Robert think it was really his idea. He knew the man so well by now, it was like writing lines for him.

"Would you mind if we had a look at your sons' bedrooms, Mrs Dillon?" Robert asked.

Nellie Dillon immediately stood aside. "Not at all," she replied.

Robert and James made their way up the heavily carpeted stairs.

"There's just the two rooms up there," she called after them. "Do you want me to come up and tell you which is which?"

"Not at all, Mrs Dillon. We'll figure it out, I'm sure," James answered.

On a dressing table that had seen better days, there was a cross, a holy picture of Christ, and a silver candlestick complete with a white wax candle. There were several pairs of rosary beads laid out side by side.

"This is the failed priest's room," Robert guessed.

"Looks that way, alright," James agreed.

"Father Pat's altar," Robert said. "Did he say mass, I wonder?"

James was staring at the beads.

"See anything you like?" Robert said jokingly.

James picked up a pair of pearl beads.

"Nice choice," Robert cajoled.

"These are real," James announced. "Real mother of pearl."

"You mean they're not plastic."

"Worth a few pounds, these are," James said, nodding.

"So, where did he get them?"

"You'd only get these in a jeweller's," James suggested.

The rest of the room threw up nothing else of interest, so they made their way to the room next door.

"What's with the carpet on the stairs? Looks new," James remarked.

"I would say it's been laid on top of another one. Stair carpets aren't usually that thick," Robert replied.

"At least she wouldn't hear the two boyos descending or ascending," James said.

"A blessing, if you're a light sleeper," Robert said.

"So, this is the famous Dick's room," James said.

"It would appear so, seeing it's the only other one up here. Such a tiny house, claustrophobic."

Nothing of note surfaced as far as Robert could see, but as he prepared to leave the room, James caught him by the arm.

"What is it, James?"

James dropped to his knees and looked under the bed.

"Mind there's not a piss pot under there, Jamey lad," Robert said, and laughed.

James pulled out a tin case.

"What treasure have we here?" Robert asked.

James opened the case to reveal an array of watches, clocks, silver candlesticks, and a velvet box containing silver cutlery.

"Jeweller's stuff," Robert said, nodding.

James held up a large wad of fifty-euro notes. "And look at this little pile, sir," he said.

"Now, that is either the jeweller woman's dough, or their employers'. How much do you reckon there is, James?"

"At a rough estimate, I'd say a few thousand," James replied.

"That much." Robert was surprised. "I hardly think the jeweller woman would have that kind of money at her place. She couldn't be making much in the shop. Unless, of course, she doesn't use the bank and keeps it all on the premises instead."

"Should we talk to the employers first?" James ventured.

Robert made for the door. "Employers, definitely first," he answered.

"What'll I do with this, sir?" James asked.

"Put it back where you found it, and we will deal with it later," Robert said, then left the room and made his way down the stairs.

Mrs Dillon approached him the minute he landed in the hall, and he couldn't help noticing she looked fairly anxious.

"Thank you for being so accommodating, Mrs Dillon," he said, with a smile.

"Don't mind your blooming Mrs Dillon, call me Nellie like everybody else does. Well, not everybody, some do call me Mrs Dillon but..."

"Nellie, that's a nice name, is it a shortened version of Ellen or Helen?" Robert asked, interrupting. Nellie the elephant had crossed his mind, but she was hardly named after the said elephant, he thought.

"Eleanor, actually, is my full name. Strange the way a lot of us aren't called by the name we were christened. Nicknames and shortened versions become the norm. Dick's real name is Richard, and Pat's is…"

"Patrick," Robert interjected.

"That's a lovely carpet you have on the stairs," James stated as soon as he joined them. He had done a last-minute spot check of both rooms.

"It was a gift," Nellie replied.

Robert was already heading for the front door, which slightly irked James. He would have liked to have done a bit more probing.

The carpet was a gift, that sounded interesting. From whom? he wondered.

"Come on, James," Robert called over his shoulder.

"Nice to have met you, Mrs Dillon," James said.

"Nellie, though I'm really Eleanor. I told him already, he will tell you if you ask him."

"I'm sure he will when I ask him," James said.

He would be asking no such thing, because he knew he'd been told not to be bothering with idle tittle tattle which bore no relevance to the case. Everything bore relevance to the case, but how could you get that across to an impatient man, James wondered.

CHAPTER 12

"This is like something out of a Charles Dickens novel," James said in an exaggerated ghostly voice as he and Robert surveyed the mahogany panelled walls.

The floor was a sea of even darker wood, and the ceiling, not wishing to be left out, was more of the same. It was like they'd just stepped into a very large timber box.

"Will you look at the grandfather clock? This is just like the old curiosity shop. Any minute now, Little Nell and her grandfather will make an appearance." Robert stifled a laugh as soon as he made the observation.

How many trees did they have to kill to kit this place out, James was about to remark when the opening of a door right down the back distracted him.

"So, you are not too impressed with our premises."

Nothing wrong with this old gent's ears, Robert thought as he made his way towards the man he presumed to be Mr Kelly.

"I'm Detective Inspector Carroll," Robert said as he held out his hand. "And this is my assistant, James Sayder."

Robert realized his offer of a handshake was not going to be reciprocated, so he dropped his hand to his side and tried not to look too bothered by the rebuff.

"I know who you are, at least I now know which one is which."

"Bring them in," a voice called out from inside.

"This is my brother Bob, and I'm Jack, by the way. We have no curiosities here to sell, we just deal in cider. Yellow in colour, made from apples."

The dig did not register with Robert, and James felt he had to apologize on his boss's behalf.

"Sorry about that, a bit of a stupid remark on our part, but I'm sure you will understand we are all a bit wound up over what's happened to the Dillon brothers. Please accept our sincere apologies, no harm meant," James said.

If Jack was the thinnest man on the planet, his brother was the polar opposite, James thought as he turned his attention to the two Kelly brothers. Fatman and Needleman would be good nicknames for them. He would share his thoughts with Robert later. But then again, maybe not.

"We want to talk to you about your employees, or should I say, past employees, Dick and Pat Dillon," Robert began.

"That Dick fellow was a right article, pulling all sorts of scams. We couldn't prove it, of course; you know how it is."

"Was he stealing money?"

Needleman delegated himself to be spokesman. "Just bottles of cider he knocked off, which were all probably sold on to his old cronies at a bargain price. But he'd still make enough out of the deal. A right smart lad, that one, up to all sorts of shenanigans, and as for his docile brother, he went along with everything to save himself from getting a beating."

"So, how did Mr Dick manage to account for the missing cider?" James asked.

"He'd make out he dropped a crate and all the bottles broke, which they would do if you actually dropped them."

"That was clever," Robert remarked. "Any other stuff?"

The fat man took it upon himself to answer the question. "Look, we don't want to be upsetting ourselves, what's done is done."

"Would the scamming they were doing amount to something like a few thousand euros?" James asked.

"A few thousand euros!" Needleman laughed.

"Our accountant is on the ball, he would have spotted that kind of discrepancy, wouldn't he?" Fatman nudged his brother.

"He would indeed. You want to see the questions he asks about the petty cash," Needleman said.

"What happened to the box of biros you bought last month is his favourite," Fatman said, and laughed.

"Are you writing memoirs, he asks – bloody sarcasm. And we're taking that kind of abuse and paying for it," Needleman said.

"The only thing that's saving him from getting the boot out the door is he's cheap." Fatman winked.

"What we are trying to do is build up a picture of how much the boys were disliked," Robert said.

"Everyone hated them. But there's one who really hates them now," Needleman said, taking the reins.

"Who's that, then?"

"Counsellor John Hanton."

"Why's that?" Robert asked.

"Well, now, here's the thing. The discovery of their bodies is holding up the works that the good counsellor fought so hard to get for the town. Considers himself a hero, no less," Needleman expounded.

"It will be held up until the matter is resolved," Robert said.

"And that could take years, according to our esteemed counsellor. As far as he is concerned, you two are like the Keystone Cops," Needleman said, grinning.

"What a cheek," Robert retorted.

"He said you two couldn't catch a cold." Fatman added insult to injury and didn't hide the fact he thought it was funny.

"Would you mind telling us where this gobshite lives? We haven't questioned him yet, have we, James?"

"No, we haven't, sir," James answered.

Needleman scribbled the address down on an envelope he retrieved from the wastepaper basket and handed it to James.

"Do you know what, James? The Dillons were right to rob them two fucks, Laurel and fucking Hardy, up to the eyeballs," Robert said when they finally emerged out onto the street.

* * *

When Robert and James arrived at the counsellor's residence, Robert was still fuming.

James opened the gate and immediately came to the realization that they'd walked in on a huge row.

The counsellor's wife was roaring out the top window. "Get out of here, you two-timing toad."

"Ella, you don't understand, let me explain."

An array of suits and shirts came sailing through the air.

"Those are Armani suits and Ralph Lauren shirts," James remarked.

"Now, take your stuff and piss off to your pommes frites bitch."

The counsellor groaned as he tried to turn his key in the front door. "What's wrong with this bloody lock?" he said.

Then the truth hit him, there was no way his key was going to work because the lock had been changed. It had been a hasty job too, judging by the chisel marks on the surrounding timber.

"What are you playing at, you silly cow?" he shouted upwards.

"I'm going to take you to the cleaners, you cheating pig! And I'm not talking about the ones who do your suits."

The curtain next door twitched. Counsellor John Hanton glared at the figure lurking behind it with a cordless phone to its ear. "Relating everything to one of your old cronies? You nosey old bag, with your one foot in the grave. Get your other one in, 'cos you'll be no loss," he roared and made rude gestures with his finger.

Robert pointed to the net curtain with the flying ducks pattern. "It's worse than Old Macdonald's farm," he said, nudging James.

Seething with rage, John Hanton gathered up his clothing and made his way down the path. It was only then that he spotted Robert and James.

"What do you two want?" he asked. He swept past them and dumped his belongings into the boot of his car which was parked outside. On hearing the front door opening, he rushed back into the garden. "What have you done to your hair, Ella?" he asked.

"Highlights, Mark did them for me, and he changed the locks too."

"He should stick to hair locks," the counsellor said with a sneer.

"I've got a job as a barmaid. So now I can do without you and the paltry few pounds you expect me to manage on."

"Barmaid? You can't even pour a bloody cup of tea, never mind pour a blooming pint."

"Now piss off before I call the law." Ella scowled.

"They're already here, but I doubt they will be of much use to you." The counsellor gestured towards Robert and James.

Ella brought her hand out from behind her back. "Don't forget this," she said.

The counsellor watched as she aimed the object at him.

She did not miss, he realized, as he hit the ground with his head reeling from whatever it was that was after striking him.

"You've hit me with a brick and you've probably caused me brain damage, you silly woman. I'll end up in a wheelchair," the counsellor moaned.

Robert and James tried not to laugh when they saw the offending object lying a short distance away.

"It's just a block of chocolate, which is ironically called death by chocolate," James said.

"He's some drama queen." Robert laughed.

James put out a hand to help the counsellor up, but Robert ordered him to stop.

"Best phone for an ambulance, we don't want to be accused of doing anything untoward," Robert said.

James took out his mobile phone and dialled the appropriate number. He hoped that no poor deserving person was going to be done out of care while they attended to this overreacting idiot wriggling on the ground. There was something about the snivelling man that he didn't like.

"Sneaky fucker, calling us the Keystone Cops. Maybe we should help him up and give his arm a bit of a twisting," Robert said.

"As you quite rightly said, sir, no point in getting accused of anything untoward. Wouldn't be worth it," James said.

Counsellor John Hanton wiped the drool from his mouth with the sleeve of his jacket, and wished for a swift and sweet holy death. Oh, the embarrassment of this, he thought when he heard the ambulance siren in the distance. Every bloody man, woman and child would be laughing at him before the night was out, and that witch next door with her one foot in the grave would take pleasure in spreading the news, the miserable old gossipmonger, he thought.

CHAPTER 13

Doctor Morris made a hasty departure after imparting the news that the Dillon boys had been shot. On further examination, he had discovered bullet holes in both their skulls, and if he was not mistaken, according to the size of the bullet holes, they had more than likely been fired from a small gun.

He was not one bit pleased at the way the detective had sneered at him. The young fellow was alright, but Detective Carroll was a proper pain in the arse. From now on, he would be conducting all business with the said gentleman either by phone or note, because he was not going to tolerate that rude man.

Robert turned to James as soon as the doctor was out of earshot. "If we are the Keystone Cops, then that fellow is a painting by numbers coroner," he said.

James could appreciate what a difficult job it must have been for the doctor to examine the bodies, seeing they had been dead for a while. The man should be commended for discovering the real cause of their deaths, but, of course, Robert had his own ideas on the matter, so there was absolutely no point at all in trying to stand up for the unfortunate Doctor Morris.

"Small bullets fired from a small gun, did you hear him?" Robert said, sneering. "Fucking comedian."

James nodded as if in agreement, just to save himself from one of Robert's long-winded rants.

"Ring that builder fellow and tell him to get his arse in here immediately, if not sooner," Robert said.

James took himself off to the phone in the absent Celine's office. Wasn't she the lucky one, out in Spain for herself, and not here having to put up with Robert's moods. Then, on the other hand, she might be the type of woman who would take no shit from nobody. She might be the sort of woman who would put Robert in his place, like Maggie Lehane did.

Robert sighed, he was sick of this case already. Sick of this town. Sick of everything about it. To distract himself from his negative thoughts, he stared at the blackboard. James had such neat handwriting, he noticed, so unlike his own spidery scrawl. Everything about James was neat.

Martin Hayes arrived a half an hour later. "Are you having a laugh?" he said.

"What's the problem?" Robert asked.

"You want me to search Sundays Well to see if there's bullets out there? That's like looking for a needle in a haystack, if you don't mind me saying so."

"We need to find the bullets to know what kind of gun they were fired from," Robert explained.

"But don't you have some kind of forensic team?" Martin asked.

"This is Magnerstown, not Miami for fuck sake," Robert spat.

"*Miami Vice*, I loved that on the telly," Martin said, and laughed. "They don't make them like that anymore."

"Find the whole thing amusing, do you?" Robert asked.

"You will owe me big time," Martin conceded.

"Listen here, two murders have been committed, and you, my dear fellow, will have to co-operate whether you like it or not. Else, you can be done for… What can we do him for, James?"

Martin Hayes knew by the look on James's face that he didn't know the answer. But then, maybe there was no answer, Martin thought as he proceeded to walk towards the door. Thick as he was, he knew there was such a thing as perverting the course of justice, but that hardly applied in this situation, did it. The lad was right, there was no answer, and with that in mind, he gave the door one hell of a bang as he left the room, and felt a huge sense of deep satisfaction for having done so.

"You are so right, sir, this is Magnerstown, not Miami," James said, trying to diffuse the situation. "We can only do our best on what little resources we have, and I think we are doing very well given the circumstances."

Robert seemed to calm down a bit on hearing these words.

"Right, James, chalk that up, will you, about the gun that fired the small bullets," Robert said with a grin.

Bullets in the victims' heads came from a small gun as confirmed by Doctor Morris, James wrote on the blackboard.

Robert's mood suddenly improved. "A small gun; was the doc talking about a water pistol?" he said, and laughed.

"I will google small guns tonight," James said.

"No you won't," Robert said. "Take some time off."

"If you say so, sir, I don't mind if I do."

"What I would like you to do, though, in your own time, is a check up on *The Crier*. See what kind of stuff they are churning out at the moment, see what kind of shite they are printing about the Dillons," Robert said.

"As you know, sir, *The Crier* was well ahead of the game during the Joubert murders. They knew everything before we did."

"Maggie Lehane, yes indeed. Our esteemed editor was so ahead of the game alright," Robert agreed.

James cursed himself for alluding to Maggie Lehane. Robert and herself, that is if he had picked up on the situation correctly, seemed to have had a parting of the ways. It didn't surprise him one bit though, and much as he had the greatest of respect for his boss, he could well imagine that the man would be a terribly hard individual to live with.

"How the hell that rag is managing to survive beats me. Advertisements, I would say, are keeping it going. If the two fools operating it had a brain between them, they'd be dangerous," Robert said.

James did not agree with that analogy. Mossie Harrington was excellent at the job of turning out the paper, and Joey Tyrell the photographer was gifted. He could have gone places if he wasn't so fond of the cider and the whacky backy, not that there was anything wrong with that, each to his own, as the fellow says.

"So, where do we go from here, James?" Robert asked.

"At the risk of sounding cheeky, sir, perhaps a bite to eat wouldn't go astray."

"You have the uncanny habit of reading my mind," Robert said, smiling.

CHAPTER 14

Robert's first impression of Brigit Barry was that she was an extremely pretty girl. He could see she had good skin, which was why she didn't have to plaster on make-up, he presumed. Her hair was bottle-blonde but he could forgive her for that. You couldn't blame her for wanting to look her best. She had a child whose father was dead, so, naturally she was on the lookout for someone else to take her on. Good luck with that, he thought. Not many men would be willing to take on another man's child. And even if she had it adopted, she was, as the old timers used to say, second-hand goods.

A young woman came into the room and placed a tray on the table. Tea and biscuits for the guests, Robert noted. Two china cups and saucers. He cringed. He would have felt more comfortable with a mug.

"Would you like a cup?" James said, and pushed one of the cups towards Brigit.

"No, thanks," Brigit replied.

"Shall I pour out the tea?" the young woman asked.

Brigit dismissed the woman with a wave of her hand and said, "I'll do it."

Robert picked up one of the biscuits and took a bite out of it. It was thick and wholesome, homemade, he realized.

James noticed how unsteady Brigit's hand was as she poured out the tea. He could see she was nervous.

"Milk and sugar?" Brigit asked.

"We will sort that out ourselves," James said.

"We are investigating the murders of Dick and Pat Dillon." Robert made the formal announcement.

"He made a right idiot out of me," Brigit snapped.

"You could say he's got his comeuppance then, couldn't you? So, that must make you happy," Robert said.

"He made a right idiot out of me," Brigit said, repeating her comment.

"So you've said," Robert remarked.

"I have to keep convincing myself that that's what he's done. Because, one minute I hate him and the next minute I love him."

"I know exactly what you mean," Robert said.

Brigit wiped her eyes with the back of her hand. "I am so glad he is dead. I really am delighted," she said.

"So, who would, apart from yourself, in your own words, be glad he is dead? How about your uncle? Could he have had anything to do with Dick Dillon's untimely demise?" Robert asked.

"My uncle wouldn't harm a fly. I would, though. I sure as hell would if given half a chance."

"I don't think a pretty young woman like you would be capable of doing anything bad to anybody, no matter how awful they were to you," Robert said.

"I'd harm a fly, though; dirty little buggers pitching on your food and you don't know where they've been," Brigit said jokingly.

"Tell us about Sundays Well," Robert said, smiling.

"That bloody place. I suppose you could say that's where my child was conceived. You could say it because it's the truth."

76

"Is that right?" Robert said.

"I should hate it, but I don't."

"Memories are always there to haunt you, aren't they? But maybe you might like to tell us more, all in the strictest of confidence, of course," Robert said.

"I used to have to feel my way along the edge of a rocky wall until I came to a hidden recess. I would have to crouch down to make my way inside a small cave which Dick had discovered when he was a young lad, that's what he told me, anyway. He seemed quite proud of the secret place that he and his brother frequented for years. They went there to smoke and read dirty magazines, to talk about the fairer sex, and sex. Talk about it was all they did, though, but he was hardly going to admit that to me, was he? The vagabond Dick."

"So, then the venue changed course for the brothers?"

"Yes, it became the place for just me and him. Pat had to be put right out of the equation."

"So, you and Dick had sex there?" Robert said.

"That's a bit harsh," Brigit replied.

"Sorry, I am inclined to be a bit heavy-handed," Robert said. "Let me rephrase my question, you and Dick got to know one another better out there, isn't that right, Brigit?"

"When we met in the cave the first time, I was surprised he didn't have Pat trailing after him, considering they were joined at the hip. There is a name for those who are conjoined. I read an article about it while I was waiting for my turn at the hairdresser's. Conjoined twins, only Dick and Pat weren't conjoined technically, that is."

Brigit could see it all in her mind's eye. Dick had opened a new packet of cigarettes and offered her one that first time. She'd have been a fool if she didn't realize he was going all out to impress her.

After smoking a cigarette and a bit of small talk, the real game began in earnest. Dick did some fumbling. He put one hand down her front and the other between her legs. He was, as the girls used to say in school, like an octopus, or the other favourite description of theirs was: he was all over her like a bad rash.

It didn't take her long to figure out why Dick was without his shadow, and she couldn't help wondering how he'd actually bribed his brother to make himself scarce in order to carry out his big seduction plan.

It became a habit, meeting in the cave, and she gladly went along with it. But then, after a while, doubt began to set in, and she knew she should challenge him about all this hiding. It was true they had to have their special time in the cave because, where else could they go? But this business of telling nobody about their relationship didn't sit well with her.

Dick said it was better meeting in secret, because it made it far more exciting. Like forbidden fruit, he'd said. Wouldn't she agree? He'd keep asking until she'd nod her head.

Was he ashamed of her? Was that the real reason for the secrecy? She was only a barmaid. Was that it? Did he think he was better than her because he worked in Kelly's Cider Bottling Company? It wasn't as if he had a great position there; all he did was fetch out crates of cider for customers and write a docket. That was the sum total of his job. So, did he think writing dockets made him an office clerk, for God's sake, or an accountant even, for that matter?

There were times when she could knock his block off, especially after the cold ground had frozen the arse off her. Wouldn't you think he'd take off his coat and put it under her for protection? Oh no, Dick was a selfish prick and never in a million years would he think of acting the gentleman.

Robert broke in on her thoughts. "We are trying to establish if the boys were killed out in Sundays Well," he said.

"What difference does it make where they were killed?" Brigit said.

"Does your uncle possess a gun, Brigit?" Robert asked.

"He has a rifle. He kills rabbits with it. He used to try and make me eat the poor misfortunates. He said they tasted just like chicken, but I couldn't bear the thought of eating a little bunny."

"Seeing you knew the Dillons so well, who would you say could hate them so much that they went and killed them?" Robert asked.

"That young one's father," she replied.

James knew exactly who Brigit was alluding to, but he kept quiet. Best not to let Robert know he was ahead of the game, because Robert would only think he was trying to upstage him.

"What young one?" Robert asked.

"Marie McGrath."

"Yes, of course."

"You know her?"

"We both know her," James blurted out.

Robert shot him a look.

"Are you going to tell me not to leave the country, and hand over my passport? Not that I could do that, because I haven't one," Brigit said, and laughed.

"Here's my card, and if you can think of anything at all that might help us in our enquiries, we would be most grateful," Robert said.

"And have you got a card?" Brigit asked, looking straight into James's face.

James wanted to admit he didn't have a card because he was only the helper after all. According to his uncle, he was a babysitter, and if Robert knew that, he would go absolutely mad.

"Do think about it, won't you, Brigit? You surely wouldn't want the killer of your child's father to escape scot-free," Robert said.

"You haven't touched your tea," Brigit said.

"I prefer coffee, but the biscuits were very nice, though," Robert admitted.

CHAPTER 15

"James, how are you?"

James looked into Mark's face.

"You still work at Mary I's?" James asked.

The night James first saw Mark, he was sitting on a high stool at the counter in the pub with Katie Manning. They were both nurses at Mary I's nursing home.

Please, don't ask me about Katie, James prayed inwardly.

"So how is Katie?" Mark asked.

The truth, if James was to admit it, was that he didn't know how Katie was. Her phone calls had stopped in the last few months, and all he got now was the odd text. Just touching base, she'd say. Was that all he was now, a base?

"Anything new in Mary I's?" James said, changing the subject.

"You know yourself, James, all the same poor lost souls we always had lying in their beds with the clock ticking. We got a new patient a few weeks ago, though. A woman who lived on the main street. She got kicked out of her house because it got condemned."

"I heard about that, not about that woman exactly, but the kicking out of the tenants. A chap called Mossie

Harrington got kicked out for the same reason. He works for *The Crier*, so at least he escaped Mary I's, not that I'm saying there's anything wrong with the place," James said.

"Anyway, this woman I am talking about lived beside him, as it happens. I feel so sorry for her because she's quite sprightly. But she will go downhill. Being stuck in confinement sucks the life out of you. Take some people out of their environment, and it's a condemned to death job," Mark said.

"Was there no one to come to her aid? Did the council not offer to give her shelter?"

"That's a laugh. Now here's the thing, she has a daughter, but her daughter has her own agenda. She is suing the council on behalf of her mother, but that's a load of rubbish. She was probably paid off to persuade her mother to leave," Mark replied.

"By whom?" James asked, intrigued.

"Well, this old lady, my patient, told me something very interesting. Seeing you are a policeman, I feel I have an obligation to tell you."

James smiled at that. He wasn't really a policeman, just a work experience fellow. Though that job description had changed, according to his uncle, he was tagging along with Robert Carroll because the man needed guidance. Guidance – that was a good one. All the same, he felt very proud he had been called upon to participate in this investigation of the bodies in the well.

"She said she heard Martin Hayes, he's the local builder, and John Hanton, the local counsellor, arguing outside her window the day before the council told her that her house was condemned."

"Did she say what the argument was about?" James asked.

"She said Hayes was adamant the houses were sound, and Hanton reminded him that he could earn a nice sum of money if he played along."

"Does it ever end, this corruption?" James said.

"Chancers will always be around," Mark replied.

Mark's phone bleeped in his pocket. After reading the message, he told James he had to go.

James hurried up the street to the station, he was a few minutes late, but what about it. He had, after all, been furnished with information which could prove very useful in the case.

The desk sergeant greeted James and waved a note in the air when he arrived at the station.

"You may as well take this, seeing the boss is not here." The sergeant thrust the note into James's hand.

James made his way to the incident room and sat down. Dare he take a peek at the note? he wondered.

Doctor Morris had the most awful handwriting, but he could just about make it out. The gist of the thing was that there was more news about the bullets that the good doctor had found embedded in the two boys' skulls.

He now knew the type of gun that had been used in the situation. Apparently, he had called upon the expertise of a friend who knew everything there was to know about guns.

The bullets would have been fired from a small gun, as he had previously said, but now he had it on authority that the gun in question, according to this gun enthusiast friend, was a derringer.

James refolded the note and placed it on the desk where Robert usually sat, and then went back to his side of the desk, seated himself and folded his arms.

It was so quiet down here, peaceful in fact, he thought. He would savour the calm until Robert arrived because he knew that, as soon as the man read the note, he would kick off big time.

Doctor Morris would once again get a right old ear bashing in his absence. That was so unfair, really, because as far as James was concerned, the doctor was doing a really great job. But try telling that to Robert. No, he would never try telling the man anything. Just go with the flow, best way, really.

CHAPTER 16

James averted his eyes from the glass case. How anyone would want a stuffed fox in their sitting room was a mystery to him. Taxidermists had a lot to answer for. How they could do that kind of task was beyond him. It was cruelty to animals; alright, so they were dead, but that was no excuse. Imagine if they started doing that to human beings, there would be public outrage.

"That is your property, is it not?" Robert asked.

Miss Kneeshaw barely glanced at the contents in the cardboard box.

"I expect it is," she replied.

"The money, is that yours too?" James intervened.

"No, the money is not mine."

"We will have to hold on to it so," Robert said.

James, taking the hint, removed the money and stuffed it in his pocket.

"Can you do me a favour?" Miss Kneeshaw said, addressing James.

"Of course," James answered.

"Could you please take the box out to the shop. You will see a drawer under the counter; if you could just tip the stuff into it, I would be grateful. You might tear up the box, if you don't mind. I have a recycling bin in the corner."

James picked up the box and made for the shop. Older people were so much better at recycling than the younger generation. Now, where had he heard that? he wondered as he carried out the instructions.

"I am wondering why you haven't asked us where we located your property, Miss Kneeshaw," Robert said.

"The Dillons stole it," Miss Kneeshaw replied.

"So, you knew?" Robert said.

"Does Mrs Dillon know you found it? I presume it was hidden in the house somewhere," Miss Kneeshaw asked.

"No, she doesn't know we found it. It was in Dick's bedroom as it happens, but we managed to keep it from her. At least I think we did."

"She didn't know what those two scallywags were up to half the time," Miss Kneeshaw said.

"You are very fond of her, aren't you? And you wouldn't want to hurt her," Robert said.

"She has the key to this place, that's how they got in. They took it without her knowing, sneaky brats."

"Would I be right in thinking you didn't press charges against them because you didn't want to upset her?" Robert asked.

"I feel so sorry for the woman. She had a hard life with her two sons, and that father of theirs. He was a drunkard. A selfish man who didn't appreciate the woman who made so many sacrifices."

"Have you always lived here?" Robert was asking Miss Kneeshaw when James returned. She looked a bit annoyed, Robert had obviously managed to get on the wrong side of her. What insensitive thing had he said to her? There were times when Robert sounded a bit too pushy when he was interviewing people, which didn't go down well with the misfortunate at the other end.

"All done and dusted," James said.

Miss Kneeshaw acknowledged James's presence by nodding at him, and then she turned her attention back to Robert. Looking him square in the face, she said: "Well, now I reckon you know all there is to know about me. Someone will have queued up to inform you about the German Jew who came riding into town with her father to take over the place."

She was right about that. The desk sergeant had imparted all he knew about Miss Kneeshaw. He hadn't referred to her status, though. In fact, he was very much in praise of her. He said she was an expert at fixing watches and clocks, and that her many customers were grateful for her service at such a low cost. She was an unsung hero as far as they were concerned.

"My father got out of Germany on time, unlike many others. I owe my life to his bravery," Miss Kneeshaw said, with a sad smile.

"You must have only been a child when you came here, but you adapted, like children always do," Robert remarked.

"My mother refused to come with us, and she ended up in the gas chambers for her folly."

"That must have been heart-breaking for your father, and for you too, I would imagine," James said.

"It was hard for my father leaving her behind. She was always stubborn, he used to say when I asked him about her. He didn't tell me about the way she died until years later. You know, sometimes he used to blame himself for not forcing her to come with us, but he always finished up by saying, sometimes you have to take drastic measures, even if it hurts someone, to survive."

"We will take our leave," Robert said as he stood up.

"Nice to have met you both," Miss Kneeshaw said.

"Likewise," Robert replied.

James felt they should stay on and let the woman talk. He got the impression she was in need of a listening ear. She had worked herself up to the point of disclosing some personal information, which must have been a huge thing for her, and obviously she had more to give.

Robert was out of the door like a shot, James noticed. There were times when he wondered if the man had any heart at all.

"Nice to have met you," James said.

"He's a sad man, isn't he, that boss of yours," Miss Kneeshaw said.

"I'll come and visit you sometime, if you like," James offered.

"That would be nice."

James had to run up the street to catch up with Robert.

"Managed to tear yourself away, did you?" Robert said.

James decided this was one of those times when it was best to remain silent. No comment should apply.

"I couldn't be listening to that dribble," Robert said.

No comment, James thought.

CHAPTER 17

"You look really nice, Lilly," James said, smiling.

"You sound surprised, did you expect me to be wearing my white shop coat? No, let me rephrase that, my off-white shop coat," Lilly said, with a grin.

"So, what can I get you?" James asked.

"Cocktail of the day, or should I say cocktail of the night?" Lilly replied.

James made his way to the counter.

"I see you are with my sister," the barman said.

James looked back to where Lilly was sitting. "Lilly is your sister? She never said."

James felt slightly uncomfortable. Did she think she needed a chaperone, was that the reason she suggested this pub?

"So, what's it to be, then?"

"Cocktail for Lilly, and Coke for me."

"We don't do drugs here."

James laughed, even though he didn't think the joke was in the slightest bit funny.

"I'm Gerry Larby, by the way."

"And I'm James Sayder."

"I have to be truthful, I know who you are," Gerry said. "You are one of the detectives investigating the bodies in the well."

"Famous in my own lunchtime," James smiled.

"Ah, that's an old one," Gerry said.

"I am not one bit funny," James admitted. "But you are good. Ever think of pursuing a career in the comedy business?"

"I've enough careers on the go without adding another one." Gerry set the two drinks down on the counter.

"So, what's that cocktail called?" James asked.

"It's called a slippery nipple, and you'd better not get any ideas from it," Gerry said.

James put a ten euro note on the counter and hoped it would be enough to cover the two drinks. He knew these cocktails cost a fortune.

"The look on your face," Gerry howled with laughter.

Lilly tapped James on the arm. "Is he winding you up? I thought I'd better come and rescue you," she said.

"He is just educating me in the art of cocktails," James said.

"The latest thing is a double port and a WKD," Gerry said.

"Isn't that something to do with cricket?" James asked.

"It's actually a blue drink, and it's pronounced wicked." Lilly pushed James playfully.

James picked up the two drinks and told Gerry to keep the change, if there was any.

"He is such a pain, my darling brother," Lilly said when they seated themselves back at the table in the corner.

"He's alright," James replied.

"My grandfather, the one and only Mr George Larby, owns this pub and a carpet business, and the corner shop.

But I told you that already, did I not? Or maybe I didn't, but you know it now." Lilly smiled.

"Does your brother work in the carpet business as well?" James asked.

"Laying carpets by day and laying drinks down on the counter by night. That's our Gerry for you," Lilly said.

James managed to make his fizzy drink last all evening, because he knew from past experience that he would be having to get up to go to the bathroom all night if he overindulged.

"Have you got no homes to go to?" Gerry bellowed at the end of the night.

"We needn't go," Lilly said, and winked.

As soon as the bar was cleared, not that there were many other punters, Gerry joined Lilly and James.

"I am so tired this minute," Gerry said, and yawned.

"I don't know how you do it," Lilly said. "I feel hard done by with the long hours I do in the shop, but at least that's all I have to do."

"So, how is the investigation going?" Gerry asked.

"You know he can't answer that," Lilly said.

"Only making small talk," Gerry added.

"Couldn't you talk about something else?" Lilly snapped.

"I think we should call it a night, let your brother get on with his clearing up," James suggested.

"I like you, James," Gerry said.

"You certainly have your hands full, Gerry. Could we help you to get the place sorted out?" James asked.

"What's with the 'we'?" Lilly said, and laughed.

"Tomorrow morning, I have to fit three carpets. They've all gone mad getting new carpets. It's like carpet season," Gerry said.

"It must be back-breaking. I could never do it," James said.

"You have to take up the old carpet and, you know, some of them are almost glued to the floor, so there's all that scraping to be done."

"Nothing is easy, is it," James said.

"If you could fit a carpet on top of an old carpet, that would be grand alright," Gerry said.

James laughed at the idea of it.

"I did that very thing, believe it or not," Gerry said.

"Are you saying you fitted a carpet on top of an old carpet?" James asked.

"Exactly. I did it for Miss Kneeshaw, as it happens."

"And she gave him a big tip, didn't she, Gerry?" Lilly said.

"There was some carpet left over and she asked me to fit it up Mrs Dillon's stairs. Poor Mrs Dillon's stair carpet was threadbare, so there was no point in removing it. You could say it acted as an underlay. Miss Kneeshaw's carpet wasn't that bad, but she insisted I lay her new one down on top of it."

"That's interesting," James said.

"It wasn't cheap either, Axminster it was."

"A lady with good taste," James said.

"Rotten with money she is, and I didn't really deserve the whole of the tip," Gerry said, and smiled.

"Would you get many tips?" James asked.

"God, no. Plenty of complaints though, you'd get, but as for tips, no. They're like rare birds."

"Don't go on about the dead Brown Booby that was found in Cork last year," Lilly said, warning her brother.

"Are you a birdwatcher?" James asked.

"I used to dabble a bit in the bird breeding game, but I had to knock that on the head with all the work I have to do, I just didn't have the time no more."

"So, tell me about the complaints you get in the carpet business," James said.

"Let me see. The number one peeve is, are you sure that's the one I picked out? It looked different in the

92

showroom. Then there's the big old insinuation that the carpet is thinner than the one they have chosen, and the suggestion that we are running some kind of scam," Gerry said with a scowl.

"I suppose a discount would be asked for," James asked.

"Usually, yes, but my grandfather is the one who deals with it, and no more is said," Gerry said, and laughed.

"Tough, is he?" James asked.

"He don't put up with shit," Gerry replied.

"You said you didn't deserve the whole of the tip Miss Kneeshaw gave you. Why was that?" James asked, prompting.

"The new carpet was already down on top of the old one when I arrived, all I had to do was fit it in place."

"Grandad started the job, but he couldn't finish it on account of his back. He suffers with pain when the weather is damp. Arthritis: Ireland's pain," Lilly explained.

"Are you sure we can't help you clear up here?" James asked.

"Not at all, I'll be grand," Gerry said, smiling.

"Lilly, we'd better make ourselves scarce. We should let your brother get on with it, else he will be here all night," James said.

"Straight home now, no detours," Gerry said, and laughed.

"I'll follow the map," James said.

"Do you have an atlas in your pocket?" Gerry laughed.

"Night, Gerry," Lilly said.

James waved goodbye. "It was nice meeting you, Gerry," he said.

"Same here," Gerry replied.

CHAPTER 18

Robert placed his nightcap on the bedside locker and eased himself in between the sheets. His old shoulder injury, which he had acquired when he was working on a farm in France, suddenly reared its ugly head, and much to his annoyance it was giving him gyp all day long.

According to an article in a health magazine someone had left behind in the lounge downstairs, a change in the weather could bring on pains and aches. He'd only picked the bloody thing up and leafed through it to kill time while waiting for James to make an appearance. Normally, he wouldn't be a fan of health magazines, all mumbo-jumbo as far as he was concerned, with their new-fangled ideas which were in fact old ideas dressed up with new names, like mindfulness, and all that kind of bullshit. However, the information about the reason for pain at certain times of the year did strike a chord with him.

There had been an early morning frost for the past few days, and the coat he'd brought with him wasn't exactly warm enough for these kinds of elements. He didn't think there'd be frost this early in the year, but weather nowadays was so unpredictable. All down to climate change, according to the experts, which in his opinion was another load of old tosh, but what was he doing working himself up into a tizzy when he should be staying calm and enjoying a bit of peace and quiet in private.

He took a grateful sip of his beloved brandy and laid his head down on the pillow. The bed, he had to admit, was extremely comfortable. The receptionist had informed him that all the beds in the hotel had been replaced a few months ago. Some business grant from the government was apparently the reason for the big revamp. The sheets and duvet covers were Egyptian cotton, she said. He hadn't a clue what Egyptian cotton was, nor did he want to know, but the linen did feel really cool and comfortable.

The knocking on the door interrupted his train of thought.

Probably James; he cursed the fellow under his breath. Does he ever go off duty, he wondered as he threw on his dressing gown and made towards the door.

"Is this John Hanton's room?"

She was quite a striking woman, Robert couldn't help thinking as he laid eyes on the tall, willowy lady standing outside in the corridor.

"If this is John Hanton's room, I'm going to be done for trespassing," Robert said, and laughed.

"111, that's the number he gave me."

Robert pointed to the number on the door. "That's what it says, but I'm afraid you must have been given the wrong number."

"I should go down to reception and check, but I'd rather not. She's such a nosey witch, I would prefer not to draw attention to myself."

Robert took the hint. "Would you like me to ring reception and ask what his number is. It would be no bother at all," he said.

"Thanks."

"Come in, no point in you standing out there drawing attention to yourself." Robert couldn't help getting the dig in. She wasn't very charitable this one, with her name calling.

Robert pressed the R button on the phone.

"Can you tell me what room John Hanton is booked into?" he asked.

He was told that was confidential information, and therefore it could not be divulged under any circumstances.

"I am a detective and, for your information, it is vital that I am told his number, if you don't mind," Robert said.

Apologies were made. She was standing in for the usual receptionist who was off tonight and she hadn't realized who he was when he buzzed down. The room number was immediately disclosed.

Robert put down the phone.

"I should have introduced myself. I'm Robert Carroll and, yes, I told the receptionist the truth, I am a detective."

"You are here because of the bodies in the well."

"That's right."

"I'm Hanne McGrath."

Robert held his hand out. "Pleased to meet you."

Hanne ignored his gesture.

"The number you want is 101," Robert said.

"I do hope you are not going to tell people that I came here to meet John Hanton," Hanne said.

"I don't do gossiping," Robert replied.

"Sure."

"What you do is your own business."

Hanne turned to go.

"Is there anything at all that you might be able to tell me about the murders, a favour for a favour," Robert asked.

Hanne turned around with a quizzical look on her perfectly made-up face.

"I don't mean you had anything to do with the situation, but sometimes people know things that can be useful, if you see what I mean, and that can be very helpful to us," Robert explained.

"My daughter Marie hated them, maybe you should ask her."

"I have already, as it happens, met your daughter, and I don't think she would be capable of killing them," Robert admitted, then continued, "Not in her condition, poor girl. She told me she got polio in Belgium."

"Blame me for picking up the disease, did she? The spiteful little cow," Hanne said.

"No, she didn't put any blame on you at all," Robert said.

"She is not the sweet innocent little girl you think she is. She was always making up things about those boys. She has a twisted mind, she's a liar, always was."

"You don't believe she was being bullied?"

"If anyone's a bully, she is. She hated them so much, I am sure she had something to do with their deaths."

"I am afraid I just don't believe that."

"She got someone to do her dirty work for her, she's good at that."

"Like who?" Robert asked.

"She has her father wrapped around her little finger. He'd do anything for her," Hanne said vindictively. "He'd kill for her."

"You are not suggesting…"

"You're the detective, you find out."

Hanne made for the door.

"Goodnight; nice to have met you," Robert called after her.

As she banged the door behind her with venom, Robert regretted having been so accommodating to her. What a lousy excuse for a human being, he thought. It was clear she hated her daughter, and her husband too. She was the female version of Judas, hanging her daughter and husband out to dry.

What a performance she gave. She must have thought he was a complete idiot. She was the one who was doing wrong. It was obvious she was having an affair with John Hanton. For the love of God and all that's holy, what on earth did she see in the geeky boss-eyed freak?

What does anyone see in anyone? Robert mused as he returned to his bed. He removed his dressing gown and threw it on the chair.

Then he took a grateful gulp from his glass and instantly felt better.

This was his medicine, but he would have to take it easy, he told himself as he eased his body into bed.

He lay back on the pillow willing himself not to let thoughts flood his head, but he knew he would fail miserably, so he would have to refill and refill until sleep eventually came.

CHAPTER 19

James looked on from a short distance away as Marie McGrath peered into the well. It wasn't as if she was going to see anything, but she did so want to come out here for reasons of her own. He didn't have the heart to refuse her when she asked if he would help her.

"So this is where they ended up," Marie said.

"Do you know the history of this place?" James asked.

"It's called Sundays Well. The clue is in the word Sunday."

"Sunday would be a day for mass. So, does that mean a priest would perform the sacrament out here in the olden days, was that it?" James asked.

"That's right, but there's another story which I am more inclined to believe. The townsfolk used to come out here on a Sunday and throw coins into the well. Sunday being the day of rest, so to speak. You would need to find something to do, I suppose, seeing everything in town would be closed down for the day."

"They could have had picnics out here. I say out here, but it's only on the verge of town – a ten-minute walk," James said.

"The town would have been much smaller in those days, so this would have been further away then," Marie replied.

"Yes, I'd imagine this place was the highlight of the week in its time," James said, and laughed as he walked over to the well and stood beside Marie.

"I wonder if they will continue with the plan to make this place a tourist attraction," Marie said.

"Now that it has acquired a reputation, it will be all the more attractive in a ghoulish sort of way," James replied.

"Some bright spark will see a way to make money, and will probably come up with the idea for murder mystery weekends," Marie suggested.

"Are you glad the Dillons are gone?" James asked, changing the subject.

"They gave me such a hard time, they were just pure bullies, always going on about my iron leg."

"Ignorance is bliss, they say," James said.

"I was so embarrassed when I met you first, ashamed of what you might think of my affliction," Marie said.

"There's more to a person than their physical appearance. I just see you, Marie, and you are a very intelligent young woman. It's a pity those bullies were so cruel to you, but they are gone now so you need to worry no longer."

"I didn't wish them dead though, much as I hated them, I didn't wish that on them," Marie said.

"No, you'd be too kind-hearted for that."

"I see the blue and white tape has been pulled away," Marie said.

"I'd say a few sightseers were responsible for that."

"They love the macabre, don't they, as you quite rightly said. Ghouls and goblins, murder and mayhem is all the rage."

"There is a market for it alright, and I think the murder mystery weekends are definitely on the cards."

"Who killed them?" Marie asked.

"That's what we have to find out."

"You must have some idea," Marie said.

"Would you have a suspect in mind yourself, Marie?" he asked.

"Me? Sure, what would I know?"

James spread his hand across the top of the well.

"Were they thrown in? Did they drown? There would be water down there in the bottom of the well, wouldn't there?" Marie said.

"You know I can't tell you that," James said apologetically.

"I know you are a busy man with more important things to be doing than standing here listening to me rattling on," Marie said.

"It was my pleasure," James said.

Marie walked ahead towards the car that the desk sergeant had kindly loaned to James. He had told the man why he wanted it, and he was only too happy to oblige.

"Careful there," James said.

It had been raining the whole of the previous day and the ground was very muddy in places. James stood for a minute, taking in the scene.

"I'll be with you in a minute," he said, calling after Marie.

The tape was broken as Marie had pointed out, but that wasn't unusual in itself. There was something else he spotted, there were muddy car tyre tracks, which went all the way up to the well.

He went back to take a closer look. There was mud up the side of the well that he hadn't noticed until now. It looked for all the world like someone had taken something out of the boot of a car, pulled it towards the well, and then hauled it up the side.

Something had been dumped in the well. He would have to tell Robert immediately, he thought as he dialled his boss's number. As usual, it went straight into message. Did the man ever answer his phone? He left a message.

Marie invited James back to the chipper for a fish and chip supper to thank him for the favour.

* * *

James tapped on Robert's door when he got back to the hotel shortly after eleven o'clock. Getting no reply, James decided to take his phone out with the intention of ringing Robert, but immediately changed his mind. What was the point, it wouldn't be answered anyway.

He was just turning to go when the door opened. Robert looked like he had just been dragged backwards through a bush.

"Sorry to disturb you, sir," James said.

"Come in," Robert beckoned.

James eyed the glass on the locker.

"I was having an early night, and a nightcap to ensure an early night, but never make plans, eh?" Robert said.

"Sorry to disturb you, sir," James said, apologising.

"Don't keep repeating yourself," Robert said with a bark.

"I'm sorry…"

"Get on with it, James. Sorry if I sound snappy, but my shoulder has been paining me all day," Robert said.

"I took Marie McGrath out to Sundays Well this afternoon. She wanted to see where the Dillon brothers died."

Robert eased himself into the bed and took a swig from the glass on the locker.

"I can talk in the morning," James said.

"No, fire ahead."

"I noticed something odd," James explained.

"Firstly, remind me, who is Marie McGrath?"

"She's…"

"Yes, I remember, the little one with the iron thing on her leg."

"That's her."

"She came to see me. She had questions about the Dillons," Robert said.

"They gave her a hard time, did she tell you that?" James said.

Robert took another swig. He was past caring what James was going to think of him. Past caring what anyone was going to think of him, but then wasn't he being a bit presumptuous? Nobody thought about him at all.

"Anyway, to cut a long story short," James began.

"All stories should be short," Robert quipped.

"As I said, I noticed something odd out there," James continued.

"The well is still there, is it? Nobody's gone and stolen it for a souvenir, have they?" Robert said, and laughed.

"The tape was broken," James explained.

"Your point being?"

"There were tyre marks leading up the well."

"For God's sake, James."

"All activity has stopped out there, and these tyre marks were fresh."

"Fresh, were they? Had a best before date on them, had they?" Robert said with a sneer.

"It was raining all day yesterday and the place was pretty muddy," James said, patiently.

Robert looked at his watch before removing it. Carefully, he placed it beside the glass on the locker.

"It looked to me like someone had dragged something right up to the well and dumped it in. There was mud on the side of the well," James related.

"Rubbish."

"I'll say goodnight, sir," James said.

"That's all it was, some chancer dumping rubbish," Robert said.

"Night, sir."

"See you at breakfast," Robert said.

James closed the door quietly, then looked up and down the corridor. The silence was deafening, he thought; there was more life in a graveyard.

He let himself into his room wondering if anyone actually stayed in the hotel apart from the few travelling salesmen. They booked in once a month, according to his informant, the lovely receptionist who had a thing for Robert. She'd be lucky, because Robert seemed to have turned into a cardboard cut-out.

A cup of hot chocolate crossed his mind. He would love one right now to wind him down.

He looked at the tray beside the electric kettle. There were sachets of coffee and tea. Coffee would keep him awake and tea he didn't fancy; he liked a pot in the morning but not at night.

He could buzz down to the reception and ask for a mug of hot chocolate to be sent up to him, he thought. No, he would leave the poor girl in peace.

Tomorrow, he would buy a box of those little sachets of drinking chocolate from Lilly in the corner shop, and a packet of Hobnobs. Hot chocolate and Hobnobs, a little bit of heaven in peace and quiet.

Robert had his brandy, and he would have his chocolate and Hobnobs.

CHAPTER 20

James joined Robert at the table near the window. Their usual spot had been taken up by a couple who looked like they were on their honeymoon. They were holding hands, and totally ignoring the food in front of them.

"My head feels like it's had a concrete block dropped on it from a huge height," Robert said, moaning.

"Sorry about that, sir," James said.

"No need for you to be sorry, it was self-inflicted."

"They say a greasy fry-up is a good cure for a hangover, and a couple of glasses of tomato juice," James said.

"And that is something we are guaranteed to get here," Robert said, gruffly.

The waitress smiled down at them, with her notebook in hand and black biro poised, ready for action.

"Usual, is it?" she prompted.

Robert threw his eyes up to heaven.

"The usual for both of us, and a glass of tomato juice," James said.

"If I don't get out of this bloody kip of a place, and out of this godforsaken town soon, I'll crack up," Robert said with a groan.

"Are you missing a certain somebody?" James dared to ask the question.

"No, I'm not," Robert said with a scowl.

"Sorry, sir, none of my business."

"Now that you've brought her up, she'd be furious if she knew that those two latchicos she left in charge of *The Crier* are sitting on their hands. The harmless report of the bodies in the well. And that headline was so childish," Robert said.

"Ding dong bell, pussy's in the well." James laughed. He did, as it happened, think it was a great title, but he wasn't going to voice his opinion to the bear with the sore head seated opposite him. Past experience had taught him that there were times when it was best to keep one's mouth shut.

"Oh, my head," Robert moaned. "I will never ever, and I really mean it…"

"Have you thought anymore about what I told you last night?" James asked, interrupting.

"Please, shut up, James. Please, don't utter another sound until I get a gallon of coffee inside me. I'm in the form for giving someone a right tongue-lashing, and there is every chance I might do it."

"Sorry," James said.

"Will you stop using that word?"

The food arrived: eggs, bacon, sausages and black pudding basking in a greasy sauna for Robert. Scrambled eggs, which were a pastel shade of yellow, for James. A rack of toast and a pot of coffee for Robert, a pot of tea for James, and a tall tumbler of tomato juice complete with ice.

James poured out his tea and took a mouthful.

"How do you drink black tea?" Robert asked.

"I have an aversion to milk in hot liquids," James replied.

"Reaction?"

"No, aversion."

Robert proceeded to cut one of the sausages on his plate into small pieces and James had to avert his eyes from the grease oozing out of it. It was enough to put you right off food for life. He studied the runny yellow mass on his own plate and decided there and then that he would fork one little morsel into his mouth just to make it look like it was fine. He could put a slice of toast over the rest of it on the plate to make it look like he had consumed it all.

"As I said, that spread in *The Crier* was embarrassing," Robert said.

James felt he had to say something Robert would want to hear and said, "Speculation, speculation, speculation."

"At least Maggie Lehane was better than that," Robert admitted.

"Will she come back to resume her former role, do you think? If not now, maybe sometime in the future?" James asked.

"Back to this sleepy town? No, I don't think so. Maggie Lehane has seen the bright lights and she is hooked."

"Would you live here again, sir?"

"In Magnerstown? Not in a million years, my dear James."

"I actually like it here," James said.

"You know something? I think this hotel should be declared unfit to operate," Robert said, complaining.

"It's the only place in town where you can stay, apart from that Bed and Breakfast down the road," James said.

"What's it called, Ach nah what?"

"Ach nah Sheen."

"So, what's that in English?" Robert asked.

"Achnasheen is a small village in Scotland, according to a certain search engine. Don't know how the crowd here in town came up with it, but I could ask them, if you want to know," James offered.

"That wouldn't be number one on my need-to-know list."

"The thing about B&Bs is you don't have much privacy, and they don't have a bar, if a bar was something you'd be looking for," James remarked.

"I'd feel claustrophobic, at least. As you said, there are a few extras here, bad as it is," Robert said.

The smell and look of the excuse for food on Robert's plate was making James queasy, so in order to distract himself he asked a question. "So, what's next on our agenda?"

Robert downed a cup of coffee and promptly refilled it.

"Is everything alright for you?" the waitress said, appearing out of nowhere.

She had never asked that before. What was she up to? James wondered.

"Are you any good at finding missing persons?" she whispered.

James felt he had to say something, seeing she was looking directly at him. "Depends," he said.

The waitress looked around as if she was making sure nobody was within earshot. Then she divulged that a guest had gone missing from their room.

"Gone off without paying the bill?" James asked.

"Counsellor John Hanton, it is," the waitress said.

Robert came to life. "The fellow whose wife threw him out."

"Him, yes."

"The wife probably rang him to tell him she was taking him back, so he hightailed it back in case she changed her mind," James said.

"Can we have another pot of tea over here?" The smiling couple was calling.

"He could have done a runner with his lover," Robert said.

"A lover," James said, and laughed.

"Didn't I tell you about my encounter with her?" Robert asked.

"No, but you can tell me now," James replied.

"She mistook my room for his, said her name was Hanne, something or other. I was a bit inebriated, if you get my drift. No, I remember now, McGrath, Hanne McGrath."

"Queen Hanne of Belgium," James said, and laughed.

"I don't know what you are talking about, but if it makes sense to you, James, then it's alright," Robert said.

"That explains it all, wife and lover in pursuit of our esteemed counsellor. He's done a runner alright," James said.

"Wife and lover, the ugly bugs ball of a man, what do they see in him, for God's sake," Robert asked.

"There was a gossip columnist called Dorothy Parker who had a lot to say about ugly men," James said.

The delegated spokesperson for the smiling couple repeated their request for another pot of tea.

"They have had two pots already and not poured out one drop," the waitress said with a snarl.

"Don't mind them, just bring me another pot of coffee, and I would be very happy if it was a bit hotter this time, if that's not too much of a tall order," Robert said.

James cringed.

"I will make it myself, and it will be so hot you will wish you were on the Titanic when the iceberg hit it," the waitress replied.

James couldn't help but admire the waitress. She certainly put Robert in his place. How did she and her counterparts put up with it, slaving over disgruntled guests? No way could he work in the hospitality business; he wouldn't last five minutes. He would be shown the door pronto, because as soon as somebody complained about something, he would lose his head. If he came up against someone complaining about something not being hot enough, he would just dump the replacement into their laps. Hope that's hot enough for you, he'd say into their shocked faces. But would he do all that? Of course he wouldn't; but no harm in thinking that he might be brave enough.

"She is some cheeky mare, that one," Robert said.

James nodded in agreement because he felt he had to.

"Did you notice anything?" Robert asked.

"I noticed a lot of things," James said, and laughed.

"I deliberately said that about the McGrath woman calling to my room looking for Hanton. It pays to put the cat among the pigeons. Hope our little waitress spreads the news, which she will, of course," Robert said, grinning.

The call went up once more from the honeymoon table. "Where's our tea?"

"Do you hear that hen-pecked fuck," Robert said.

"I hear him, loud and clear," James said, smiling.

The waitress tapped the new bridegroom on the shoulder. "I'll bring two pots this time, one each, how about that?" she said.

"She's good," James remarked.

"You asked me what was on the agenda for today," Robert said.

"I did indeed, sir."

"I am too sick to even function, so I am going back to bed, simply because I have every faith in you keeping calm and carrying on, James," Robert said.

"No problem."

Robert picked up the tomato juice and took a slug.

"You know something? This is nice," he said.

"A bloody Mary without the vodka," James said, and laughed.

"Don't be putting ideas into my head, aren't I bad enough? Now I'm off and you won't see me until I feel human again."

CHAPTER 21

"Mrs Hanton, I wonder if you and I might have a quick chat," James asked.

"Your face looks familiar, have we met?"

"Not officially, except I was here the day you..."

"The day I threw that two-timing yoke out, I remember now, you were with that other fellow with the grouchy face."

"My boss, Detective Inspector Robert Carroll."

"Come in, I can see from the corner of my eye that that woman next door is on duty. Valley of the squinting windows, this place is."

James stepped into the hall.

"I have just made a pot of tea, and a batch of scones are cooling down, if you would like to join me?"

"Sounds right up my street," James replied.

"Sit down, make yourself at home."

James stared at the spread on the table. Crème and raspberry jam in little pots and the most luscious looking scones he had ever seen were displayed on a cake stand.

"Like what you see?" Mrs Hanton asked.

"Need you ask?" James said.

"I am living it up, because my husband is the meanest old skinflint of all times. He thought nothing of using up stale bread; made great toast, he would always say when he was living here. I can't believe I've finally got rid of him."

James savoured every morsel of the first scone and all the trimmings, and then the second washed down with Earl Grey tea, before declaring the reason why he was there.

"Your husband, John Hanton," he began.

"Please tell me he is dead."

"No, I can't tell you that, but what I can tell you is, he is missing."

"The council offices rang me, I must admit, wanting to know if he was sick or something, because he hadn't turned up to do whatever it is he does there."

"So, what did you tell them?"

"I could have said he's gone off with his bit on the side, but I didn't want to sound like the embittered wife."

"He seems to have done a runner from the hotel," James said.

"Well, as I said, he has probably gone off with that woman."

"No, he hasn't," James said.

"Let me get my head around this, you are saying that he has done a disappearing act, is that it?"

"Looks like it," James replied.

"Well, he hasn't come grovelling to me, so where is he?"

"Mrs Hanton, I would appreciate it if you didn't mention to my boss that I came here to see you. He might think I am losing the run of myself operating behind his back, if you get my meaning."

"I'm good at keeping secrets," Mrs Hanton said, and smiled broadly.

* * *

"If I could have a word, sir," James said when he met Robert at breakfast the following morning. The honeymoon couple had departed, so they got their usual table, which seemed to please Robert.

Robert eyeballed the pot of coffee and the glass of iced tomato juice. "I feel there is a request coming on, James. Best spit it out so I can enjoy my hangover cure in peace," he said.

"I know you think my theory is a load of rubbish, sir, but if you could just indulge me this one time."

"I am listening," Robert said.

"Could we get Martin Hayes to have a look down the well? Just for the purpose of elimination, if you get my drift."

"You are like a dog with a bone, James." Robert sighed.

"I met Mrs Hanton in the post office yesterday and I told her that her husband has done a runner from the hotel. Then, I asked her if he had returned home by any chance."

"Did she say you were a nosy old so-and-so, and to mind your own business?"

"She was, as it happens, very interested. She told me he hadn't returned home, and here's the best bit."

"Don't keep me in suspense," Robert said with a grin.

"She said she found it odd that the council rang and asked where he was. She said, on reflection, she thought he might have gone off for a few days with his 'bit on the side'. She wasn't exactly that nice about it, not that I blame her."

James congratulated himself on telling two lies and appearing to get away with it. Well, needs must, after all. He was slightly annoyed that Robert had dismissed his theory out of hand, that something untoward had gone on out at the well. James had a gut feeling Hanton had come to an untimely end, but what would he have to do to convince Robert.

113

"I told you about the disturbance out at the well, didn't I, sir? I told you about the broken tape, the tyre marks and the mud on the wall of the well."

"To be honest with you, James, I was half cut when you called to my room."

Robert stared into the distance after James outlined his take on the situation, and James knew from past experience it was not wise to interrupt one of Robert's staring moments.

"Get it organized, James. Bear it in mind, though, that you will have to take full responsibility for wasting police time and money if you are wrong."

"I will get it organized, and take full responsibility in that order."

"He'll want payment, the smart Martin Hayes, for searching the well. Strikes me as the type who is always keen to make a buck," Robert said.

"What if we asked that Mick McCarthy fellow instead? A pint might be all the reward he'd be asking for, or maybe we could stretch to a second one," James suggested.

"No, we can't ask him. Hayes would say we went behind his back. He is the boss, after all," Robert replied.

Yes, he was the boss after all, that was true, James thought. Robert was good with the old sly dig, but this was a double dig.

James knew Robert thought he was a bit too smart for his own good, but he always tried so hard not to give the man reason to dislike him.

Robert poured out a cup of coffee and did his usual milk and sugar additions. He took a huge gulp from the clinking glass, and then picked up his coffee.

"Now, James, I don't know about you but I am absolutely starving. I could eat a small horse and ask for seconds," he said.

CHAPTER 22

Martin Hayes resurfaced from Sundays Well looking like someone who had just seen a ghost.

"Spit it out," Robert demanded.

"There's something down there alright, and it's wrapped in plastic," Martin said.

"Small, medium, or large?" Robert asked.

"Large. I don't want to jump the gun, but I think it's a body," Martin replied.

"For the love of fuck," Robert said with a groan.

James felt a sense of relief. His hunch was right, so he was not going to get a bawling off about wasting time and money. A bit of praise wouldn't go astray, but there was fat chance of that. Robert didn't like one-upmanship, not that that had been the intention.

"Right," Robert said. "Listen to me, you two."

James and Martin looked at Robert.

"This time we do it by the book," Robert said.

Martin Hayes took out a packet of cigarettes and opened it with shaking hands. He held the packet out to Robert.

Robert shook his head. "I've given up, yet again," he said.

"I'd say you are a non-smoker," Martin said, addressing James.

Cheeky sod, James thought as he felt annoyance welling up. Insinuating he was some sort of nerd. Why you had to smoke and drink to be a real man was something he could never fathom.

Robert held both his hands up. "Now, this time, as I said, we do it the right way," he announced.

Martin Hayes tried hard to suppress a laugh. He had heard rumours that Robert Carroll and his sidekick were nicknamed the Keystone Cops. Do it the right way, that would be a miracle, he felt like saying out loud. Better not though, the best thing was to stay on the right side of the law, he thought.

"James, you get on to your uncle and tell him we need a forensic team out here, pronto," Robert ordered.

James fished his phone out of his pocket.

"And as for you, Mr Hayes, you better keep your big mouth shut, or else we will be arresting you for compromising a murder scene."

Martin Hayes gave Robert a look. What in the name of God was he talking about? He was told to go down into the well. If that was compromising a murder scene, then why didn't the man who thought he was better than Sherlock Homes go down himself?

"Do you mind staying here until the boys arrive, James? I'm walking back to the station. I need a bit of fresh air after all this bloody shit," Robert said.

"Well, there's gratitude for you," Martin whispered to James.

"I think he meant…"

"He doesn't know what he meant," Martin said with a snarl.

James was inclined to agree with Martin, but he was hardly going to admit it. A Judas was something he could never be.

"How in God's name do you put up with him? He's giving you a bad name, do you know that?" Martin said.

"It's just his way, you soon get used to it," James said.

"Do you know something? I'd give him such a massive toe up the hole if he was my boss," Martin said.

James laughed.

"I've a fellow who thinks he's the boss. I have to keep my eye on him. Mick fucking McCarthy is his name. He thinks he's better than me. It's a cut-throat world we live in now, everyone watching everyone else's job. Everyone thinking they could do better than the one who's really in charge," Martin said.

"Right, you did good, thanks very much, Martin," James said.

"You, my dear young man, are a true gent, unlike that twat of a boss you have. You know what? You should be the boss, not him."

"I prefer to muddle along, makes life much easier," James said, smiling.

"Do you want me to stay here in case I'm needed?" Martin asked.

"No, it's alright. The fellows who are coming will have their own ways and means," James said.

"You mind yourself now, and don't take no guff from him, do you hear me?" Martin said before hurrying away.

James looked at his watch. Hopefully the boys in the white suits would be there before dark.

CHAPTER 23

James looked at the number coming up on his mobile phone. It was his uncle calling, he realized. He had expected this, Robert was being bypassed.

The forensic findings would be faxed to Magnerstown Garda station, marked for the attention of Detective Inspector Robert Carroll, just to keep him happy, and Doctor Morris would be perfectly capable of doing the post-mortem and report. A brief synopsis of the findings was rattled off, and finally came the request not to ring anymore with happenings in that dead-end town. Fair enough; James offered assurance he would adhere to the request, and then the line went dead.

James lay down on his bed and mulled over what he had been told. According to forensics, the plastic sheet the victim was wrapped in contained wool fibres, which were identified as having come from a carpet. The victim had been shot in the head, and the bullet was still embedded in the skull. Death was more than likely a result of loss of blood. The victim was lying on the sheet on a carpeted floor when he got killed, was the suggestion.

So, why was he lying on the sheet on a floor? James wondered. The killer hardly said lie down there while I shoot you, and the victim hardly complied.

The best bit was, the killer didn't bother removing the victim's identity. His wallet was still in his pocket. And the victim was, indeed, the one and only Counsellor John Hanton.

But why dump him in the well? The killer would have known that John Hanton would be found if the revamping of the area went on. But would it go on with the main man out of the way? So many questions, and so few answers.

James awoke at six o'clock, still fully clothed.

* * *

James arrived at the hospital mortuary feeling awful.

"I have just got a copy of the forensic report," Robert informed him.

"That's good," James replied.

Doctor Morris smiled at James. "We must stop meeting like this," he said.

James mustered a laugh. Doctor Morris was a great man for the clichés.

"It's Hanton," Robert said.

"Good lord," James said, feigning surprise.

"Bullet from a small gun in the head," Doctor Morris said, taking centre stage.

"Go on," Robert said.

Doctor Morris produced a silver bowl containing something that looked like a marinade for meat. "Our man here had consumed a cocktail of alcohol and sedatives before he died," he said.

There's the answer then, James thought. He wasn't asked to lie down on the plastic sheet, he more than likely slid down onto it after drinking the lethal cocktail. Hardly a slippery nipple like the one Lilly likes to drink. But would he not have wondered what the plastic sheet was doing on the floor in the first place? Why would it have been there?

Why had he not suspected something was afoot and made a run for it? Why didn't he detect the sedatives in the drink? Well, you wouldn't then, would you? Not until they actually worked. Why did he accept a drink in the first place? Was it someone he was used to socializing with? Was it a woman he knew, or one he didn't know?

"According to the forensic report, there were wool particles on the plastic sheet," Robert said. "What do you make of that, James?"

"Now, here's the thing," Doctor Morris said.

"So, what's that then," Robert asked.

"If I might make a guess."

"If you must," Robert said.

"We could be looking at the same gun that killed the two boys. No, I will stake my life on it, we are looking at the same gun that killed all three."

"So, what would the Dillon brothers and Counsellor Hanton have in common, I wonder?" Robert asked.

"That's for you to find out," Doctor Morris said as he removed his purple plastic gloves and binned them.

"Thanks, Doctor, you have been very helpful," James said.

"Yes, I suppose you have, Doctor," Robert admitted.

"Now I'm off to prepare my master chef dinner for tonight. I am entertaining a guest," Doctor Morris said, and laughed.

"Oh, what are you having?" James asked.

"Spatchcock chicken marinated in peri-peri sauce; it's all the rage now. I lobbed it into the fridge this morning. The longer it's marinated, the better it is."

"You can get sachets of peri-peri sauce. I've seen them in the supermarket. You just put the chicken into a plastic bag and add the sauce," James said.

"Oh God, no. I make my own," Doctor Morris said.

Robert eyed the contents of the silver bowl and had a disgusting thought.

"I expect you will be visiting Mrs Hanton to tell her the good news," Doctor Morris said.

"That's a bit insensitive, isn't it?" Robert said with a frown.

"She's a good-looking woman, she will have a queue of suitors lined up at her door, I bet," Doctor Morris said.

Robert laughed as he and James stepped out onto the street. "Do you think the good doctor will be at the front of the queue at the widow Hanton's door?" he said.

"He is still the same, always chasing some lady," James said.

"Spatchcock, yeah, how apt," Robert said.

Was that Robert's attempt at making a joke? James wondered.

"There will be no spatch, but plenty of the other thing," Robert said, and laughed.

"How old would you say he is?" James asked.

"He's well into his sixties, but what's that got to do with anything," Robert said.

"I didn't mean…"

"Only pulling your leg, James. Now, let's go and get a decent mug of coffee, and I quite fancy a chunk of carrot cake. Then we will go and deliver the sad, or happy news to Mrs Hanton," Robert said.

CHAPTER 24

"I know what you've come to tell me," Mrs Hanton said.

"So sorry for your loss," Robert said.

"That's what she said too, but I put her straight."

"Who?" Robert asked.

"A social worker, she said she was, you've only just missed her."

"You mean you already know…"

"That he was found in the bottom of the well, yes, I know," Mrs Hanton replied.

"It's standard procedure for a liaison officer to visit the next of kin, and as we don't have one at the station, a social worker is the next best thing," James said.

"Did your husband have enemies, Mrs Hanton?" Robert began.

"Do you have a week to spare, and at least ten notebooks to jot down all the names?" Mrs Hanton replied with a wry smile.

"We have plenty of time to spare, and we can send out for a few more notebooks, apart from the one James has in his pocket," Robert said.

James took the hint and fished out his small notebook and pencil.

"You do know the good man was instrumental in getting those houses between the jewellers and the chipper condemned," Mrs Hanton said as a matter of fact.

"Can you elaborate on that, Mrs Hanton?"

"Two of the people who lived in the houses had to resort to going into the nursing home. Those poor misfortunates, imagine having to give up the place they spent their lifetime in – heart-breaking."

"Was it Mary I's they went into?" Robert asked.

"The very place," Mrs Hanton confirmed.

"The third man got a heart attack and died; all that stress, not good at all having all that drama foisted upon you when you have got on in years."

"And the fourth man?" Robert prompted.

"He was lucky his employer allowed him to live in her house."

Robert knew who she was referring to, but he felt he had to ask anyway. "So, who was this fourth man?" Robert said.

"Mossie Harrington."

"Forge Cottage is the place where this Mr Harrington is now residing, I do believe," Robert said.

"That's right."

"So, let's get this straight: your husband had an ulterior motive for having the street closed down, am I right in saying that?" Robert asked.

"Yes, he wants the whole street closed down, or should I say he wanted, to use the correct terminology, now that he is himself past tense."

"For what purpose did he want the street condemned?" Robert asked.

"A supermarket, would you believe."

"Was he going to build a supermarket?" Robert asked.

"A supermarket crowd wanted to open here in town, and they were going to give him four million notes for his pains."

"That's a lot of dosh," Robert said, and laughed.

"It certainly is."

"That left Miss Kneeshaw the jeweller and Con McGrath in the fish and chip shop to deal with. So, how was he going to buy them off?" Robert asked.

"He had a direct line to Con McGrath's wife, and I wouldn't put anything past that woman," Mrs Hanton said, smiling sardonically.

"Hanne McGrath," Robert said.

"Do you know her?" Mrs Hanton asked.

"I met her briefly," Robert replied.

"She'd do anything for money, that one. He probably promised her a few thousand quid if she managed to persuade her husband to sell up and go."

"You have been most helpful. We might be calling on you again, if you don't mind," Robert said, indicating the interview was over.

Mrs Hanton took a copy of *The Crier* from the kitchen worktop and threw it down on the table. "By the way, have you seen this?" she asked.

'Counsellor Knee-deep in Conspiracy to have Street Demolished' was the bold headline.

"Could I borrow it?" Robert asked.

"You may keep it, what would I want it for?" Mrs Hanton said, snapping.

"Notice anything?" Robert asked when they left the house.

"Indulge me, sir," James said.

"She never mentioned the affair her husband was having."

"Oh yes, what was it she said before she hit him with the block of chocolate that day we called to the house?" James said.

"'Fuck off to your pommes frites bitch,' or words to that effect," Robert replied.

"No, sir, it was piss."

"What!"

"She said piss off to your..."

124

"She is probably ashamed, poor woman; ashamed that her geek of a husband strayed from the fold. Her confidence has probably gone underground," Robert said.

"Low self-esteem is the term used, sir."

"Coffee, James. My self-esteem is in danger of exploding."

* * *

"Gerry tells me you have a new boyfriend, Lilly, love."

"No, he is not my boyfriend, just a friend."

"He's a man, and men aren't friends."

"Maybe that was the way it was in your day, Grandad."

"So, who is he, this new man of yours?"

"His name is James Sayder."

"That detective fellow."

"You are well informed of the goings on."

"So, what does he want with you, Lilly? Funnelling for information I would imagine would be his purpose."

"You are so suspicious, Grandad."

"I have never trusted detectives or anyone to do with the law."

"All they do is try to get information out of a person. Yes, I hear you loud and clear," Lilly said, annoyed.

"Sneaky yokes."

"I like him," Lilly said.

"If you say so."

"He was very impressed about you owning three businesses."

"Was he now?"

"He said Gerry was a great man to be doing two jobs."

"If it wasn't for me, Gerry would be lying in bed all day. He would be twiddling his thumbs like all the other lazy good for nothings in this town who wouldn't work their way out of a paper bag. He probably would even be on drugs."

"I know that, Grandad, and I know you really motivated him. He was so depressed after Dad died, and then Mam dying two years later really had a terrible effect on him. We would not have survived without you, Grandad, and don't think for one minute that we don't appreciate all you've done for us," Lilly said.

"Despite what you think, I worry about Gerry. Sometimes, he goes for days without opening his mouth. He has no friends whatsoever. That can't be normal, can it?"

"He seemed to get on great with James. He told him all about carpet laying. I was surprised he opened up so much to a total stranger."

"Is this James fellow going to order a carpet from us?"

"He is staying in the Dobbyn's Hotel, so he is hardly in need of a carpet, unless of course he persuades them to re-carpet the whole outfit," Lilly said, and laughed.

"I don't know how they get away with it in that excuse for a hotel. The punters must be nose blind. The smell of those musty carpets, old as the hills. I tried persuading them to get the whole place carpeted out, but they didn't think it was number one on their priority list. They got new beds though, I suppose that's a start."

"Gerry was kind of showing off, really. He was going on about some of the clients' little idiosyncrasies," Lilly said.

"What do you mean?"

"He was telling James about Miss Kneeshaw, for instance."

"What about her?"

"Well, he was saying how he fitted a carpet for her, and she wanted it down on top of the old one, and the offcut she wanted to be fitted up Mrs Dillon's stairs."

"For the love of Jesus."

"What's wrong, Grandad?"

"That is a breach of trust."

"Breach of trust, for God's sake, it's only a carpet, Grandad, not a blooming state secret!" Lilly spluttered.

"That brother of yours is too mouthy for his own good. Always was, and so are you, for that matter, Lilly, always mouthing off."

"What on earth are you talking about," Lilly said.

"You are probably blabbing to that detective fellow, telling him all our business. No wonder he is hanging around with you."

Lilly was surprised by her grandad's outburst. What was so wrong with what Gerry told James about Miss Kneeshaw and her eccentricity? And what was he going on about saying she was telling James things, and that's all he wanted her for? What an insult, she thought.

She was just about to voice her opinion, when he suddenly jumped up and stormed out of the house, leaving her wondering why on earth he was after getting so upset, and more importantly, where he was going.

She hoped his destination was not the pub to challenge Gerry.

CHAPTER 25

James pointed to the article on the front page of *The Crier.* "Will you just take a look at this bit, sir," he said.

"Tell me, I haven't the patience."

"Firstly, it is Mossie Harrington who has written the piece."

"Oh yeah, the multi-talented Mossie. Go on," Robert said.

"According to Mossie's report, it seems Martin Hayes, our esteemed builder, had connections with Counsellor Hanton."

"Yes, we know that, the refurbishing of the well. Thought that he was coming out with breaking news, did he? Mr Journalist of the Year," Robert said.

"Oh no, there's much more than that, according…"

"Look, let's stop wasting time on the fairy stories that comic is squandering good ink on," Robert said dismissively.

Robert clearly had a problem with Mossie and the newspaper, James realized. Don't ever mention *The Crier* again, James scolded himself.

It was good information though, James couldn't help thinking, and it was such a pity Robert wasn't prepared to put his resentments aside and listen to it.

"Con McGrath would have a grudge with the counsellor. Write that up on the board with the red chalk," Robert said.

"Would that be on account of John Hanton having an affair with Con's wife?" James asked.

"How do you know that?" Robert asked.

"I deduced she was. Remember the day Mrs Hanton was throwing him out, she said 'now piss off to your pommes frites bitch'."

Robert agonised for a minute, did he tell James about Hanne McGrath knocking on his door and declaring she was looking for John Hanton's room? He couldn't remember, for God's sake. What was happening to him? These memory lapses were bad news. He would have to ease up on the drink before he forgot his own name, he thought.

James searched through the box of chalk. There was green, yellow, white, and even blue, but not one stick of red.

"If someone had an affair with my wife, that is, if I had a wife, I would want to kill them," Robert said.

"There's no red chalk, sir," James said, lamely.

"Get some in the newsagents later. Prime suspects we highlight in red," Robert said, divulging his big idea.

"Yes, sir, I'll do that. Shall I just use blue instead of red for now? I'll make a note here that it has to be changed."

"Hanne McGrath, jot her down too. Hanton could have been calling it a day on their seedy little affair. You do know what they say about a woman scorned, don't you, James?" Robert said.

"And Mossie Harrington wasn't too fond of Hanton, either. His article was dripping acid," James said.

"Write his name down in yellow."

"Yellow, sir?"

"Yellow for people who wouldn't have the balls to kill someone."

James picked up the yellow chalk and wrote Mossie's name in capital letters. "He could be useful, sir, this Mossie fellow," James remarked.

"Alright, we will speak to him. Maybe we might get something of value out of him," Robert conceded.

"We are soon going to run out of room on this board at the rate we are going," James said, and laughed.

"The whole town has something to hide, if you ask me," Robert said.

For once, James was inclined to agree with his boss. Everyone had some dark secret; well, that wasn't fair, really: some were an open book.

"What's the population of this town," Robert said, wondering aloud.

"Six thousand or thereabouts, sir," James replied.

"You'd want an awfully big board for that load," Robert said, grinning.

"And a thousand sticks of red chalk," James said.

"You sure would, and we would be bypassing the newsagents and going direct to the chalk factory," Robert said.

"And think of all the people we would be keeping in a job!" James said, and laughed.

Robert shot James a look.

"Sorry, sir," James said feebly.

"A bowl of soup wouldn't go astray with a few crispy rolls. We'll go to that little café at the bottom of the hill," Robert said.

"The Waterfront."

"Strange that, isn't it? Seeing there's no river here in town. Unless, of course, you count that stream running from the creamery to… where exactly does it run to, James?"

"It runs out to Dunem Woods, and then, do you know something, sir? I don't know where it goes from there."

"My stomach is rumbling. Onwards, James."

"And don't spare the horses, I know."

CHAPTER 26

Mossie Harrington squared up to Robert. "So, here we go once again round the mulberry bush," he said.

"Just trying to eliminate you from our enquiries. We are, if you would only realize it, doing you a favour," Robert said.

"So, that's it; in your humble opinion, you are doing me a favour. Remember the time you questioned me over Judge Mangan's murder? I don't think you wanted to eliminate me from that enquiry though, did you?"

"That's all in the past," Robert said.

"And if it wasn't for Maggie Lehane, you would have done me for something," Mossie said with a scowl.

James noticed Robert flinching at the mention of Maggie's name, and by the look on Mossie's face, it was evident that he'd spotted it too.

"Your little rag is still turning out breaking news, but that is debatable. And if you don't mind me saying so, you have reached a new low with the character assassination tactics."

"And what's wrong with that? Freedom of the press, surely you know all about that," Mossie said.

"According to your article in *The Crier*, you seem to have an awful lot of inside information on John Hanton."

"You can get any kind of information if you are prepared to flash the cash," Mossie smiled sardonically.

"She's trained you well, hasn't she, your ex-boss. You are still in contact with her, are you?" Robert asked.

Mossie stared at Robert. What did Maggie Lehane ever see in this grumpy old geezer? he wondered. She was not in contact with him. He had gathered that when she phoned the other night wanting an update on the doings of *The Crier*. She seemed really surprised when he told her that the brave Robert Carroll and his sidekick James Sayder were back in town to investigate the murders.

"OK, Mr Harrington, the truth of the matter is, you had a grudge against Counsellor Hanton, on account of him being the cause of you being thrown out of your house. Please don't insult my intelligence by denying it."

"Well, this might come as a surprise to you, but he did me and Sparky a huge favour, really. We absolutely love Forge Cottage, courtesy of Miss Maggie Lehane, and we don't mind staying there for the rest of our lives," Mossie said with a sneer.

That flea-bitten dog was still alive then, Robert realized, and he must be stinking the cottage out. The one thing he would never do is have an animal in his abode. The minute you walked into a place, the smell of the critters went right up your nostrils. You could shampoo them, spray all sorts of smelly things on them, but you could never mask the pong that exuded from the four-legged critters. People had to put up with the crap they produced on footpaths because their lazy owners couldn't be bothered to pick it up and bin it. The lyrics of 'Me and you and a dog named Boo' came into his head. A dog named Poo would be more apt, he thought.

"We love it in the cottage," Mossie said, breaking in on Robert's thoughts.

James wished Mossie would keep his mouth shut because he knew Robert was trying hard to contain himself.

"Hanton was a horrible excuse for a human being. He would sell his mother for money, so nobody cares about his demise. Ask around," Mossie said.

"I will," Robert answered.

At the risk of getting a dig in the mouth from his boss, James decided to make an observation. "Your article was very informative, Mr Harrington, should you acquire more information, perhaps you might be so good as to tell us first," he said.

"Why, thank you very much, that's so nice of you to say so. But then, you're the one with the brains. Yes, I will pass on anything I hear because I like you," Mossie said.

Robert went red in the face. "Get him out of here before I do irreversible damage," he muttered.

James saw Mossie to the door.

"Escort him off the premises," Robert ordered.

On the front steps of the station, Mossie tapped James on the shoulder.

"Listen, son, I know you have a lot to put up with, but she likes him, so that means we have to keep her sweet."

"Maggie Lehane, you mean?" James asked.

"What in God's name does she see in him?" Mossie asked.

"They say opposites attract," James said.

"The north pole and the south pole, you couldn't get more opposite than that," Mossie said, and laughed.

"So, let me get this straight: she knows he is back here in Magnerstown?" James said.

"She sure does."

CHAPTER 27

By the time Con McGrath hauled the last sack of potatoes out of the boot of his car, his back had begun to ache severely. He had been overdosing on the painkillers of late, and if it was possible to become immune to them, then he had; because they didn't seem to be doing the trick anymore.

The suspension of the car was crocked with all the shite he had to collect from various places. There were no painkillers for cars, though. He would just have to keep driving the thing until it clapped out. Then he would give it a decent burial, and phone David Burke to ask him to get something on the cheap.

David was working for a certain breakdown company, and he ran a small second-hand car business on the sly. He acquired these cars from some of the call-outs. "Not worth fixing," he'd tell them with the most serious face he could muster, and as soon as he saw the look of helplessness, he would offer cash to take it away. If the crowd he worked for found out about his little scam, he would be issued with his marching orders pronto. This information David had told Con one night when he knocked at the door of the chipper declaring he was starving. Con, feeling sorry for the hungry man, invited him in and offered him sustenance. David was very grateful and said if ever there was anything he could do, give him a buzz.

Con had no sooner plonked his bulk into his armchair than his daughter Marie poked her head in the door and delivered a killer blow.

The desk sergeant at the Garda station had phoned while he was out. Marie had rattled off the message. It's only a matter of formality, and there's no need to panic, all you have to do is call into the station to have a chat with the detectives in order to be eliminated from their enquiries, she reported.

This would be about the Dillon brats and Hanton the toerag, Con knew instinctively.

The week before the Dillons disappeared, he had met them down a dark alley, as the saying goes. He gave the Dick fellow a right dig into the stomach. He would have liked to have wiped the smirk off the creep's face, but he didn't want any marks showing.

He did it for Marie's sake, but he didn't tell her, and he knew the smart Dick didn't tell her either. Marie and himself kept no secrets from one another, and if Dick had told her, she would have said.

Hanne, though, was a different kettle of fish. A sneak, if ever there was one. What exactly was she doing cavorting with that gummy geek Hanton? Con had his own ideas about that. Hanton wanted the chipper, the jewellers and the houses in the middle, closed down.

Mossie Harrington had told him about the good counsellor's plans. He felt sorry for Mossie, turfed out of the house he had spent a lifetime in. He was lucky his boss let him live in her cottage, but that could come to an abrupt end if she happened to return. Where would he be then?

Con's thoughts turned to Hanne, his good wife. She had already started her serpent in the garden of Eden act.

'Wouldn't we be better off if we sold up and moved to a nice little cottage out in the country' was her latest mantra.

Was she going to get a nice sum of money from Mr Geek for her pains? Con wondered. Did the geek promise her he'd leave his wife for her?

'You can't satisfy your wife,' Hanton had said, sneering, when he had confronted him down the very same dark alley he'd encountered the Dillons in. It was like history repeating itself.

He had decided not to hit the snivelling Hanton freak, because there'd be no satisfaction in it. Hanton would only scream like a girl, and then he would go running to his two-faced sneak of a solicitor. That would be the end of the business his poor father had built up. Alright, McDonald's it was not, but it made a living, and it was security for Marie. She was a bright girl and he wanted to give her every chance. He had some money stashed away, and he intended using it for her education. His hopes were that she would go to college, make something of herself, because she was, despite her afflictions, destined for better things.

His thoughts turned back to the counsellor and he couldn't help smiling. Someone had dealt out punishment to the cross between a man and a woman and, whoever it was that had done it, deserved a medal.

"Are you alright, Dad?" Marie asked.

"I'm fine, Marie, no need to worry. I'll phone straight away and make an appointment to meet the detectives."

"You will be alright, won't you, Dad?" Marie asked.

"I've done nothing wrong, Marie, so you stop fretting now," Con said.

* * *

Robert kicked off the conversation. "We only want to have a little talk."

"Whatever," Con answered.

"Can you tell us about your relationship with…"

Con tuned out. He would call on Miss Kneeshaw as soon as he got out of here. He would warn her that there was a big unravelling job about to be done. Forearmed is forewarned, after all.

He would also have to let Mossie Harrington know that the conversation they had when he collected his fish supper on the Friday night could have been overheard.

Con thought back to the lethal conversation. Killing John Hanton had started out as a joke, but then it had been agreed that it might be the only way to stop him closing down the whole street.

We should contact Miss Kneeshaw, meet up in her place and have a serious talk about it, Mossie had suggested.

Dousing Mossie's chips with plenty of vinegar, Con had made some throwaway remark. What it was he had said, he couldn't remember exactly, but it was something to do with the way he would like to see the little toerag off.

There were times when you would be better off keeping your big gob shut. Nowadays, you can't even joke about something, because it can all be misconstrued.

Robert broke in on Con's thoughts. "You seem preoccupied," he remarked.

"Would you mind very much if we postponed this? I am tired and not feeling very well. I have this unmerciful pain in my back and I really need to lie down," Con said, pleading.

To James's relief, Robert agreed.

Con McGrath hauled himself up out of the chair and unsteadily made for the door. He had the presence of mind to close it quietly behind him.

"That was kind of you, sir," James said.

"You would want to be blind not to see that the man is fucked," Robert said.

"Yes, I agree," James said.

"Some people really get a raw deal, don't they?" Robert said.

"I agree with that too," James said.

"I was going to suggest to him that he killed Hanton because he was having an affair with his wife, but you know what, James?" Robert said.

"What, sir?"

"She wouldn't be worth doing the time for."

* * *

Marie breathed a sigh of relief when her father returned. He hadn't been arrested.

"Marie, will you please help me?"

"Of course, Dad."

"Can you get me my painkillers and a glass of water before I collapse down into a small heap?"

CHAPTER 28

James arrived at the station half an hour before the desk sergeant. He paced up and down outside until the man showed up.

"Sorry I'm late, but my alarm never went off."

"No, you're grand," James said.

"That's a lie, I forgot to set it."

"Easily done," James said.

James sat quietly in the incident room, awaiting Robert's arrival. If he could make a bet with himself, it would be that when Robert showed his face, the first thing he would come out with would be 'I thought you had gone missing.'

He was wrong.

"I know you don't like the shite they serve up for breakfast in the hotel, but you could have waited for me," Robert said.

"I didn't sleep a wink last night, sir, so I went for a walk and ended up here."

"Right, out with it."

"I was thinking about a few things, sir."

"You know thinking can be a very dangerous thing, James, but feel free to share. We have all day, after all," Robert said.

How would he explain this thing that was going round and round in his head? James wondered. He found it strange that Miss Kneeshaw had a new carpet fitted on top of the old one. He had inadvertently been given this information by Gerry, the carpet fitter. The offcut was fitted up Mrs Dillon's stairs. Was something dragged down Mrs Dillon's stairs? Was it a case of blood on the carpet, blood on the stairs?

Robert would scoff at this theory. Are you suggesting Mrs Dillon killed her sons, or are you suggesting Miss Kneeshaw killed them? What exactly are you suggesting, James? An old woman shot the two boys? For fuck sake, how would she be capable of that? Yes, that's exactly what he would say.

"You are right, sir, thinking can be dangerous."

"Did you get the red chalk?" Robert asked.

"Yes, sir, I got it."

CHAPTER 29

"We could be in trouble, Ursula." George Larby blurted the words out.

"Take it easy, George. Calm down."

"That stupid grandson of mine, I'd love to strangle him."

"Sit down and I'll get you a drink, and when you are nice and relaxed, we will talk," Miss Kneeshaw said.

Within ten minutes, George was feeling more at ease, but then Ursula always had that effect on him.

"Now, George, tell me what young Gerry has been up to that's got you so riled up," Miss Kneeshaw said as she refilled his glass.

"The idiot went and told that detective fellow he laid a new carpet for you."

Miss Kneeshaw pointed to the carpet on the floor. "And what's wrong with that? Am I not entitled to get myself a new carpet, or has it been declared a crime now?"

"You are entitled to get as many carpets as you like, but this detective fellow asked questions about it. You know, the way they can wrangle things out of you."

"What exactly was he asking?"

"Lilly told me she was out on a date with the detective fellow, and Gerry sang like a canary when they were having a bit of a lock-in. Then Mr Snoop decided to try and get Lilly to expound, the following day, I think, or was it that night. Oh look, Ursula, I can't think straight."

"It was the young man she was out with, not..."

"Yes, the young one. James something or other."

"Handsome looking creature. I knew someone like him once."

George laughed. "Are you trying to make me jealous, Ursula?"

"It was you I was talking about, you daft bat. You were like a Greek god with your shiny blond hair when you were young."

"And now I have a shiny bald head," George said, and laughed.

"So, you think the long-haired detective is putting two and two together and making five out of it."

"I hate snoops, always have," George said.

"It's his job to snoop."

"I don't think you realize the seriousness of this, Ursula."

"It will only become serious if we make it serious. So, if he comes asking, we will not give him food for thought."

"Robert Carroll is no threat at all, he couldn't catch a cold, according to the talk going around about him. But this young fellow was the one who solved the murders two years ago, according to those in the know."

"I remember Robert Carroll's father, nice man he was. It was common knowledge he had a hard time with the young Robert. He went off to France on a wild goose chase after his poor father had gone to the trouble of getting him into the guards. Not one bit grateful. I hate that, children who have everything done for them, then just throw it back in their parents' faces. Nellie Dillon was another martyr, oh how I used to pity her. She's grand now though, peace at last..."

"What are we going to do, Ursula?" George cut in.

"We do absolutely nothing, George. Do you understand?"

"You are not worried then?"

"Not one bit, and you should put your worries into an envelope and post them to Worry Land."

"I couldn't sleep the other night and I got a panic attack. I felt like I was drowning, all my life flashed before me," George said.

"Another drink?"

"I'll be drunk and I won't be able to walk out of here," George said.

"You can sleep on the sofa, wouldn't be your first time."

"She made a right idiot out of me, the woman I married. I will rephrase that, the woman I was forced to marry."

"She wouldn't be the first woman to tell a lie in order to get her man," Miss Kneeshaw said as she refilled George's glass.

"I loved you, Ursula. You do know that, don't you?"

"My father loved you too."

"He gave me the money to start my business and buy the corner shop when that bastard of a bank manager turned me down."

"My father was a shrewd man, George. He knew you had a good business head on your shoulders and you deserved a start."

"Lilly is alright, but that other blabbermouth is just like…"

"Now forget everything bad, think of the nice things. That's what I do when I feel a bit down."

"And when you feel so down that you feel you will never get up again, what do you do then, Ursula?"

"To every problem there is a solution."

"What if there's not, what if the whole thing is going to come tumbling down around our ears, what then, Ursula?"

"Don't be upsetting yourself," Miss Kneeshaw said, smiling.

"But I can't help it. I wish I could be calm like you."

"Outward appearances can be really deceiving, George."

"That pain in my chest is back again, Ursula, and it frightens me."

"It's only stress, isn't that what your doctor said? And we all know stress is brought on by ourselves, by allowing things to get to us. Do your breathing exercises when you get home, and you'll be fine."

"Can I ring you later?"

"Will they be there when you get home?"

"No. Gerry is doing the bar, and Lilly is out with that young detective fellow."

"Good, so you should get yourself into bed, and stay there safe and sound for the rest of this good night."

"I do trust you, Ursula, I always have."

"Goodnight, George, and thanks for being a such a good friend."

CHAPTER 30

Nellie Dillon was surprised to see Miss Kneeshaw hadn't opened the shop. A list of reasons came to mind. Maybe her alarm clock didn't go off, or maybe it did and she had an early doctor's appointment, or even the dentist for that matter. Then, on the other hand, she could have decided to take the day off.

Nellie made her way to Miss Kneeshaw's bedroom, it was her favourite room in the whole of the house. Today, she would be changing the sheets and pillowslips and putting a new bedspread on.

Miss Kneeshaw wasn't a fan of duvets, she preferred candlewick bedspreads. The white one with the pink trim was the one she really loved, but she had to make do with the blue one while it was getting washed and dried. Nellie always hurried the process along by putting it in the airing cupboard, and after a few days it would be warm and fresh, and back in its rightful place.

As soon as Nellie entered the bedroom, the shoebox on the bed caught her eye. What have we here? she wondered as she opened the box.

It contained the most beautiful peep-toe shoes she'd ever seen. Blue suede and really expensive looking. They were spang new, never been worn, she realized as she turned them over and inspected the soles and heels. They reminded her a bit of the shoes she wore for her own wedding. She had a pair of suede court shoes, and she'd tried to make them look different. Peep-toe was her first attempt, but one turned out bigger than the other. So then she had the bright idea to cut the whole way across the toe area. The result was exactly what she wanted. Cutaway toe shoes, the latest fashion; she knew because she had seen a pair just like them in a fashion magazine. She had been pleased with her achievement and congratulated herself on her inventiveness. However, she was soon to regret her redesigning idea on her wedding day.

It was on a frosty morning in the last week of October, and her poor toes were so frozen that she thought she was going to get frostbite. She would have done with a pair of gloves for her equally cold fingers, but there was no way she was wearing the knitted ones she possessed. They didn't look sophisticated enough.

It was a struggle to button up the second-hand tweed coat, but she managed it. So, with the child in her belly causing the buttons to almost stretch to breaking point, she said the words 'For better or worse'.

There was no better, just a whole lot of worse.

But what was Miss Kneeshaw doing with these beautiful shoes? Nellie pushed her past memories away. The poor woman would never be able to wear them on account of that club foot of hers. Maybe the shoes belonged to her mother, or it could be possible they were a present from somebody special. A viscount for instance.

Nellie looked at the box in an effort to find a clue. Even though she couldn't speak the language, she recognized it was German. Miss Kneeshaw had told her that her mother refused to leave Germany, so maybe they brought the shoes with them as a keepsake. A memory of a loved one lost.

Just as Nellie was about to replace the lid on the shoebox, she noticed the envelope on the bed addressed to Mrs N. Dillon. She opened it with shaking hands. What was this about? she wondered. Was she getting the sack, were the shoes a termination of employment present? A golden handshake, so to speak.

Nellie couldn't bear to read the letter, so she put it back in the envelope and stuffed it into her pocket. It was best to hear the bad news from the woman herself, she thought as she made her way to the parlour.

As soon as Nellie turned the doorknob, a terrible sense of foreboding suddenly descended upon her.

She stood in the doorway for a few seconds with her eyes shut tight. Something was dreadfully wrong, she knew. She had to force herself to open her eyes, and when she did, she wished she hadn't.

Mrs Kneeshaw was lying on the floor; there was a lot of blood, and that tiny little pistol she kept in the bookcase.

She didn't tell Miss Kneeshaw she knew it was there; didn't tell her she'd taken the little gun out of the drawer for a good look.

"What have you done, Miss Kneeshaw, what have you done?" she whispered.

Nellie heard a voice in her head giving orders: it could be possible she was still alive, time is vital, call an ambulance at once. She rushed to the phone in the hall. Her hand was shaking so much that she had to dial the three numbers several times.

* * *

Someone dressed in white was peering down at Nellie. "You've had a terrible shock, Mrs Dillon. Try and drink this tea," a woman's voice said.

"Are you an angel?" Nellie asked.

"I hope not."

"Where am I?"

"You're in hospital. You got a little turn. My name is Nurse Breen, by the way."

"Miss Kneeshaw…"

"Try to get some rest," Nurse Breen said.

"No, I want to know how she is," Nellie insisted.

She spotted another face looking down at her.

"Miss Kneeshaw sadly passed away. Now you must stay calm, you're not doing yourself any good getting upset," a man's voice said.

"Did someone shoot her?" Nellie asked, hoping that was what had happened. She hoped that the thing that rushed into her mind when she saw Miss Kneeshaw with her red stained hair, was not of her own doing. Why would she do something like that to herself? Why would she do something so awful.

"Detective Inspector Carroll would like to talk to you tomorrow morning. Now, in the meantime, you have to get your strength back," Nurse Breen said.

"I need to know what happened. Please, tell me," Nellie said, pleading.

Nellie could see the nurse holding out a kidney bowl and the man in a white coat taking a syringe out of it.

"No!" Nellie cried out. "Please, no."

"It's for your own good. You must trust us," the man in the white coat said.

"You are in safe hands with Doctor McMorrow. Now, let him do his job, Mrs Dillon," Nurse Breen said.

Nellie felt her whole body fizzing and then, she was floating. She felt so light, like a feather, really.

The voices sounded far away, but she could hear them clearly.

"Would you believe it, Doctor, he's still waiting outside after I told him to go away until tomorrow," Nurse Breen said.

"That's one persistent little policeman," Doctor McMorrow said.

Nellie didn't want to hear any more, she just wanted to sleep.

"Would you credit it? Here he is, coming in again," Nurse Breen said.

"Is she in good health? She hasn't had a heart attack, has she? She will be able to talk to us, won't she?" Robert asked.

"Get out!" Doctor McMorrow said with a roar.

"I'll be back tomorrow," Robert called over his shoulder as he retreated.

"Can you believe the cheek of that fellow? At least the young man with him had the sense to stay outside," Nurse Breen said.

"The shock this lady must have got, can't have been one bit pleasant," Doctor McMorrow said.

"Her two sons were found dead out in the well, and then the fright of finding the Kneeshaw woman. God, that must have been the final straw," Nurse Breen said.

"She's a tough old biddy, she'll be back to her old self after a few days' rest," Doctor McMorrow said.

"I hope so."

"We'll put her on a mild sedative, that should help her through the weeks ahead. She'll have a lot of flashbacks, no doubt," the doctor said.

"Can I tell you something in confidence?" Nurse Breen asked.

"Fire away."

"Another thing this little lady didn't know, at least I don't think anyone told her. You know, the way you are always the last to know about something you actually really should know," Nurse Breen said.

"The suspense is killing me, and we've had enough of that for one night," Doctor McMorrow said, jokingly.

"Do you remember the blonde girl who was admitted here one night? Brigit Barry was her name, at least we got that out of her."

"God, yes; she was in the early stages of pregnancy," the doctor said, nodding.

"And do you remember we asked her who the father was, and could we call him because she was so distressed and frightened," Nurse Breen said.

"She would make a great spy that little blonde bombshell, because she didn't give an inch, did she? Anyway, what happened to her?" the doctor asked.

"Her uncle got her into a place down the country; don't know why because nobody bats an eyelid about those kinds of delicate matters nowadays," Nurse Breen said.

"And if my calculations are correct, she's had the child, has she not?"

Nurse Breen pointed to the patient. "She has indeed, and there's the grandmother, and she doesn't even know it."

"Granny Nellie Dillon," the doctor said with a grin.

* * *

Nellie was still floating, not fully knocked out, she realized, because she had heard every word.

CHAPTER 31

Doctor Morris made sure he had all the details written down because he was sick to death of that Carroll fellow treating him like he was some sort of imbecile. It had also been brought to his attention by a concerned friend in the guise of the desk sergeant, that the gumshoe was making remarks about him which were not very flattering.

Did the smart-arse detective not realize that this town is like an echo? You say something to someone and it reverberates. "We have a coroner performing autopsies like he was painting by numbers," that's what the cheeky sod was saying to whoever would even bother listening to him.

It was good of the desk sergeant to relate the irritant's mouthing-offs. Just so you know, he'd winked as he made the revelation. But now that he thought about it, the sergeant did have a wry smile on his face when he said it, like he was enjoying landing Carroll in the shit.

Carroll was landing his own self in the shit. By the looks of him, he was on a downward spiral. It was common knowledge he was hitting the bottle, and it was affecting him, even though he didn't know it. Forgetting things, for a start. It had been noticed, and noted.

"Why did you have to do this to yourself?" Doctor Morris asked the corpse on the slab.

Wouldn't I get a right shock if she answered me? He laughed as the thought stuck him. Sometimes you needed a distraction to do a job like this. You couldn't afford to be soft in this game, but when you know the people you are cutting open, it becomes a bit too personal.

The tap on the door brought him back to the land of the living.

"Come in," he called.

"Good morning, Doctor Morris," James Sayder greeted him.

Doctor Morris looked past James.

"I'm on my own," James said.

James noticed the look of relief on the doctor's face and smiled. Doctor Morris clearly had a problem with Robert, and he was entitled to feel that way.

"OK, here's the deal," Doctor Morris said. "She, as in Ursula Kneeshaw, to give the lady her full title, killed herself. I have it on authority that the gun is the same one that was used to dispose of Dick and Pat Dillon, as well as John Hanton."

"Yes, I know. I got my uncle to check it out," James said.

"According to your uncle's checkie-out man, there were two sets of fingerprints on the gun," Doctor Morris said.

"Checkie-out man, I love that," James said, and laughed.

Doctor Morris jerked his finger in the direction of the recently deceased. "One set is Ursula's."

"And the second set?"

"We don't know yet, but we will have to find out who they belong to, won't we? Although that would entail checking the whole town's fingerprints."

"How can we be so sure she killed herself?" James asked.

"Never question forensics," Doctor Morris said.

"They know their stuff?"

"She bled to death, did our Ursula. Apparently, the carpet was stained with blood, as you would expect, of course."

"I have a theory," James said.

Doctor Morris covered Miss Kneeshaw's body with a paper disposable sheet.

"Well, what is it?"

"I think it wasn't the first time the carpet in Miss Kneeshaw's parlour ended up being stained with blood," James said.

"This I like, a bit of mystery. Go on."

"Well, to be correct about it, what I really mean is, I think the carpet underneath was stained with blood and she had a new carpet fitted on top of it."

"Let me work this out in my head," Doctor Morris said.

"Be my guest," James said, nodding.

"The Dillon boys were killed in Miss Kneeshaw's parlour. Shot, they bled to death on the carpet which is underneath the new carpet."

"Exactly what I was thinking," James said.

"Then, she removed them to the well and dumped them in. Ding dong bell, two pussies in the well," Doctor Morris said, and laughed.

"Except, she could hardly perform that task all on her own because, firstly, she hasn't a car," James said.

"Is there a secondly?"

"Yes, there is, and a thirdly and a fourth…"

"I got rid of my carpet," Doctor Morris said, butting in.

"Not because of bloodstains, I hope," James said, jokingly.

"I used to have a bit of rising damp in my living room. It was right under the window at the back wall. So I replaced it with a wooden floor. The guy who did the floor for me put down thick plastic sheeting before laying the wooden floor on top. He said it would be the only solution to keep the damp from coming up."

"As a matter of interest, was it the local carpet people that you got to do the job?" James asked.

"Do you know something, I was trying to figure out where I'd seen the plastic that Counsellor Hanton's body was wrapped up in, and now I know."

Robert Carroll burst in the door.

Robert shot James a look. "Why didn't you call me?" he asked.

James wondered if he should say that he had tried to call him. Should he say that he had knocked on Robert's door on and off for half an hour and got no response? That he had surmised that Robert was gone to God because he had had one of his famous binges, and a bomb wouldn't wake him? No, James concluded, he would be doing no such thing. It was far easier to take the blame for not performing a wake-up call.

"Well, if it's not too much trouble, and I do hate to be such a nuisance, but would you two mind filling me in?" Robert said with a snarl.

Doctor Morris winked at James. "I have to be somewhere else, remember I told you that, James? Oh, and by the way, in answer to your question about my new wooden floor, it was the local crowd who did it."

James had to admire the doctor for coming up with an excuse to make his great escape. He hoped that Robert would not ask where the doctor had to go, because he had no idea.

Well, the truth was, Doctor Morris had somewhere to go, and that was as far away from Robert as he could get.

Doctor Morris waved at Robert as he dashed to the door. "I'm sure your able-bodied assistant will fill you in on the present situation," was his parting shot.

Robert stared at James. "What's the story?" he asked.

"Miss Kneeshaw committed suicide," James answered.

"Suicide," Robert echoed.

"The gun she used is the one that killed the Dillon brothers, and the one and only Counsellor John Hanton."

"That is totally preposterous," Robert said.

"They say the camera never lies, except in this case, it's forensics, sir. There's no doubt about it. The interesting thing is, there is a second set of fingerprints on the gun besides Miss Kneeshaw's."

"There you go then," Robert said.

"Forensics are certain Miss Kneeshaw fired the bullet from the gun. She definitely..."

"I suppose we will have to go with that," Robert conceded.

"The second set of fingerprints were only on the barrel of the gun itself. It was like someone handled it. Maybe when Mrs Dillon found her, she..."

"You and your theories, James."

"Sorry, sir."

"Did she leave a suicide note?" Robert asked.

"No note was found, but that's not to say..."

"Yes, yes, we know all that," Robert retorted.

"It's mostly young people who commit suicide, but older people, it's not hugely common, is it, sir?" James said.

"Statistics are not infallible," Robert said.

"You would wonder what to believe, wouldn't you, sir?"

"The first thing I struggled to believe in was Santa Clause. Childhood innocence, don't remind me. I had this theory about gullibility and stupidity," Robert said.

"I know exactly where you are coming from, sir," James said.

"Wait a minute, why am I bothering with this dribble?" Robert snapped. "Come on, time for sustenance."

CHAPTER 32

Nellie Dillon awoke with a start. Her first thought was to get her head together and figure out what had happened. Her eyes watered when she thought of the reason she was lying in a hospital bed, and not a very comfortable one either, she realized as her bones creaked.

She always thought this place was nothing but a workhouse masquerading as a hospital. There were talks of it closing down one time, but the fact that they had an intensive care ward for heart attack patients, saved it. The journey to the city hospital would be too far for anyone needing immediate treatment, so that's why it got a reprieve.

Intensive care ward, that was a laugh. There was only one bed in there, and one set of equipment. Supposing two people got a heart attack at the same time, would they have to roll a dice to see who would be hooked up?

Nellie felt annoyance welling up inside her when she thought about Doctor McMorrow and Nurse Breen landing on their feet with their plummy jobs. The two of them were getting more than they were worth and carrying on regardless.

* * *

"So, how are we this morning?" Nurse Breen tapped Nellie on the shoulder.

"I suppose you could say I am as well as can be expected under the circumstances," Nellie replied.

"You must have got an awful shock," Nurse Breen said.

Nellie looked up at the miserable, thin, pale-faced individual looking down at her.

"You found the misfortunate Miss Kneeshaw. Must have been an awful sight."

This one was on a funnelling for information exercise, Nellie knew. So, who did she want to share the gory details with? Doctor McMorrow more than likely.

"Your two boys being found dead out in the well, and then Miss Kneeshaw. Such an awful lot to take in, Mrs Dillon. I really feel for you," Nurse Breen said.

Nellie squared up to Nurse Breen. "Who is this girl my son got into trouble?" she asked straight out.

Nellie knew she had the woman's attention and waited for the information to come flowing out of her beak-like mouth.

"Alright, keep your hair on. I will tell you everything, but first I have to tell you, Mrs Dillon, there was a letter found in your pocket which was addressed to you. Well, that's stupid, really, it had to be addressed to you, otherwise it wouldn't be in your pocket, would it?"

"And no doubt you had a good look at it."

"We had to open it in case it was a suicide note that Miss Kneeshaw had written. It would have to be handed over to the investigating officers, as evidence, you see?"

"Come on, spit it out," Nellie said, feeling confident now. "Where is it now, this letter addressed to me?"

"It's in the safe in my office. I had intended giving it to you as soon as you were well enough," Nurse Breen said.

"Just tell me what was in it," Nellie demanded.

"It was a kind of will, you might say. Miss Kneeshaw made a list of instructions. Firstly, the peep-toe shoes in the box on her bed are a present for you."

"Those shoes, I love those shoes," Nellie said, and cried.

"That wasn't all. Arrangements have been made with her solicitor for you to get a very large sum of money by way of support, for the rest of your life."

Nellie was stunned. "She said all that, did she, in that little note?"

"You have to call to her solicitor as soon as you can for all the details. You are going to be a very rich woman, Mrs Dillon."

"And the girl my son got into trouble, who is she?" Nellie asked.

"Brigit Barry. If you call on her uncle Billy, I am sure he will tell you where she is, maybe not immediately, but I am sure you will prise it out of him."

"Are they the Barrys who live in Rosanna Road?" Nellie asked.

"The very ones," Nurse Breen replied.

"I don't know if I could approach him," Nellie said.

"Why not?"

"He would probably give me a right rollicking for what my son did to his niece," Nellie said, cringing.

"Look, I'm sure he would be glad of a visit. You could tell him the truth. You knew nothing about it and now you want to make amends. Surely he will be glad to hear that," Nurse Breen suggested.

"Yes, you are right. I can make amends, especially now that I am going to be rich," Nellie said, and smiled.

Nellie made a mental picture of how she would prepare for her visit to Mr Barry. She would wear the peep-toe shoes, and that beautiful wool coat she had seen in the window of O'Dea's Arcade. It was two hundred euros, but she could afford it now, couldn't she? She would look like a lady, act like a lady, and arrive in a taxi to the Barrys' house. And surely he would be so impressed, he would co-operate immediately, she thought.

CHAPTER 33

Lilly was about to lock up for the night when a customer came running in.

She listened to the woman's long-winded story about stale bread and sour milk and wasn't it the luck of God that her son, who was destined to be a scientist when he grew up, had spotted it on time.

Lilly was tired and all she wanted to do was just drag herself home and have a nice mug of hot comforting chocolate before falling into bed.

She served the customer and saw her to the door. She turned the sign from open to closed and switched the light off, just in case some other customer with a destined-to-be-a-scientist son tried to get in.

Gerry had gone off to a warehouse in the city to order some new stock, and he was staying overnight in a Bed and Breakfast, so it would be only herself and Grandad at home tonight.

Grandad wouldn't mind her having an early night because he would have his nose stuck in one of his vintage car magazines, and be glad to be left in peace.

James had sent her a text earlier, asking her to meet up, and she'd texted him back saying she just wasn't up to it. He understood, he had replied to her text.

Marco the Italian man would be doing the pub tonight, so at least she didn't have to slot in there.

She ran all the way home like she was competing in the Olympics. Usain Bolt would be so proud of her, she smiled wryly.

"I'm home, Grandad," she called out.

She made straight for the kitchen and took a carton of milk from the fridge.

Getting no reply, she concluded he was out. Probably down at the showroom, fussing over everything. He didn't entirely trust Gerry.

She'd leave a note on the table telling him she was so zonked out she had to hit the sack. She could expound by saying that, if she collapsed on the floor, he would have to scrape her off with a Stanley knife, but no need for overkill.

It's the little pleasures in life that mean the most. She smiled as she cradled the mug in her hands. She sipped the magic potion slowly, savouring it until the very last drop was gone.

She rinsed the mug under the tap and placed it in the dishwasher. She didn't have to go to that extreme, she knew, but old habits die hard. It was Gerry who had fought for the dishwasher, and Grandad had eventually given in.

That's the thing she liked about her brother, he was far more modern than her. Was he happy with his lot, though? Did he have different ambitions? She never really asked him, now that she thought about it. They were like two ships passing in the night.

Lilly made her way to the stairway to heaven. Bed. Sheer heaven awaited her, but she was so wrong.

He was lying at the bottom of the stairs, and it took her a minute to get her head into gear.

She knelt down beside him. He was still breathing, she discovered. She hurried back to the kitchen and dialled for an ambulance on the main phone.

"It's my grandfather, please come as quickly as you can," she screamed.

* * *

"Is there anything I can do?" James asked when he joined Lilly in the little room off the intensive care ward.

Lilly burst into tears.

James put his arm around her.

"Shall I ring your brother and tell him what's happened? He will probably want to come back immediately."

Lilly struggled to compose herself. "No point, what can he do? Let's wait and see how things pan out first," she said, sobbing.

"Your grandad will be alright," James said.

Nurse Breen appeared at the door.

Lilly took a deep breath. "Is he..."

"He is asking to see you."

"Do you want me to wait?" James asked.

"You go back to the hotel. I'll text you if I need you," Lilly replied.

Lilly was shocked to see all the colour had drained from her grandad's face, and he looked so small lying there hooked up to a machine that was bigger than himself.

"Lilly, Lilly, I have to tell you something."

* * *

The long night had turned into morning by the time Lilly emerged from the hospital. She had been ordered to go home and get some rest with the promise that she would be rung at once if things changed for the worst.

But things had changed. Why did he have to tell her all that stuff about Miss Kneeshaw and himself?

Why did he have to tell her that he loved Miss Kneeshaw, and he had been fooled into marrying her grandmother, who, according to him, was a scheming conniving so-and-so who had done him out of marrying the one he really loved.

The one he really loved. She was a murderer, for God's sake! How could you love a woman who was capable of killing two boys? How could you help her dispose of the bodies?

If that wasn't enough, Miss Kneeshaw then went on to kill Counsellor Hanton. This time she'd enlisted his help before the operation. Maybe she could forgive him for helping the woman to dispose of the bodies after the act, but to be present when Hanton was killed was unforgivable.

He admitted he had provided the plastic sheet and placed it on the floor, because there was no point in ruining a brand-new carpet. How callous can you get? He was there when she did it, her grandad, watching the whole thing unfold, and not doing one thing to stop it. He made it clear he agreed with the killing of Hanton. The man was a parasite, he said, a parasite who had hounded people out of their homes for his own gains. He wanted the whole street shut down for his own greedy reasons.

Miss Kneeshaw had good grounds to kill all of them, so that made it alright, did it? Lilly had fumed inwardly rather than voice her opinion to the sick man who had just confessed all.

They were stupid boys the Dillons. Daubing swastikas with red paint on the front door of the jeweller's shop. But no, Miss Kneeshaw didn't make allowances for them, because even though she was a child when she lived in Germany, she was aware of all the humiliation foisted upon her and her parents, and she never forgot it.

Ireland had become a place of refuge for her and her father, and she was damned if she was going to accept that kind of behaviour at this late stage of her life from two ignorant louts.

There were other reasons she hated them so much, one being she didn't like the way they were taunting Marie McGrath about her affliction.

They were scum, they robbed and plundered all round them. They got a lot of money from Hanton to do their tormenting.

They called her names that night they landed in her parlour. She asked them why they were tormenting their downtrodden mother. It incensed her when they made it clear they had no respect for the woman who had slaved over them all her life.

But how could you compare the Dillons with what went on in Germany? They were just your average bully boys. Why not ignore them, Lilly had dared to ask the man who could be lying on his deathbed.

Miss Kneeshaw chose to fight back. She was a hero, like the one in *The Avengers*, the brave Honor Blackman, fighting injustice, and that, according to George Larby, was the long and short of it all as far as he was concerned.

Miss Kneeshaw was an avenger, he'd said with pride. Are you deluded, Grandad? she had wanted to ask. She really wanted to rubbish all that clap trap he'd spouted out, but she didn't want to cause him any more stress. She didn't want to be the cause of him dying, because guilt was a terrible burden to carry.

Lilly realized she had a dilemma on her hands.

Should she give James Sayder all this information? She would feel like a Judas if she sold her grandfather for forty pieces of silver, not that there would be any silver involved.

What a bloody mess, Lilly thought, as she shivered in the cold morning air. She owed her grandfather a lot. He'd brought her and her brother up after their parents died, and that can't have been easy for him.

On the other hand, he had it well out of them with the work they did for him. She, slaving away in the shop until an ungodly hour of the night, and Gerry having to work in the carpet store by day and pub by night. So, who was it who said slavery had been abolished? Slavery was alive and well and still operating in Magnerstown.

Lilly pulled the collar of her coat tightly around her neck and made her way home.

CHAPTER 34

James wiped the blackboard clean and put the chalks back into the wooden box. "There we are, all done and dusted," he said.

"I wouldn't be too sure about that," Robert said.

"The case is solved, sir."

"Not as far as I am concerned," Robert said, with a frown.

"The case solved itself, you mean."

"Don't you start," Robert said.

"Miss Kneeshaw shot herself with the same gun that killed the Dillon boys and John Hanton, isn't that evidence enough?" James asked.

"You are forgetting about the second set of prints on the gun?" Robert said.

"They were only on the barrel, she fired the bullets, unless you think somebody held…"

"She was a frail old woman, so how did she dispose of the bodies? She doesn't have a car," Robert reasoned.

James had expected to meet Robert on the stairs back at the hotel with his bag packed, ready to hightail it out of town, but instead, here he was in the incident room drawing things out.

"That's true, she couldn't have done it on her own," James said in agreement.

What James really wanted to say was, Miss Kneeshaw did the murders, called in a favour for the body disposals, and who could refuse a dear old lady.

"We are looking at accessory to murder," Robert said.

James wondered if he should phone his uncle and ask him if he could have Robert told in no uncertain terms that the case was closed, and he would be physically removed from town if he didn't comply.

"Are you listening to me?" Robert barked.

"Yes, I am listening to your every word, sir."

"Someone has to be charged."

James could read Robert like a book. He knew what was really bothering him. Everyone in town had been going on about the Keystone Cops, and Robert wanted to have one up on them by finding an accomplice. As if that would make a difference. Good riddance to bad rubbish, the old adage was being bandied about in every establishment in town in relation to the three victims.

The Crier even had a cartoon on the front page. James thought it was very funny. Three cats sitting on the edge of a well, and two dogs with magnifying glasses looking up at them.

"Con McGrath is my number one suspect," Robert said.

"Why's that?" James asked.

"Remember, Hanton wanted him out of his chipper business, and the Dillon brothers were bullying his daughter."

James decided the best thing to do would be to humour the man. Just help him to get it all out of his system and then they could go home.

"Right, so Con McGrath is in the fray, you think? His wife was having an affair with Hanton," James said.

"Good point, James. There's the motive. Chalk that up, James."

James stared at the box of chalks for a minute. "What colour shall I use?" he asked.

"He has a car that could have done the job quite easily. Nice big boot in it for lugging potatoes from wherever he gets them, and a body could weigh…"

"Since you put it like that, sir, perhaps you have a point," James said, interrupting.

"We will hang on a bit longer, James. It ain't over till the fat lady sings."

"Whatever you say, sir." James managed to sound enthusiastic.

Sometimes he wondered if he was pursuing the wrong career, drama school could be a much better option, but then he was going to be a lawyer, and you definitely needed acting skills for that.

"Anything going on with *The Crier*?" Robert asked. "Any big revelations that we don't know about?"

"Our mutual friend, Joey Tyrell, is doing a bit of drawing. Cartoons. He's good too, I have to admit," James answered.

"Cartoons, for God's sake, the whole thing is a joke. Can't understand how they keep going."

"They do a lot of advertising, that kind of thing pays well," James said.

"Right, I'm off for a coffee transfusion."

"I'll catch up with you, sir, just have to make a quick phone call," James said as he scrolled through his contacts. His uncle would give him a right ear bashing, but if the man came up with the goods, as in to tell Robert the game was over, it would be well worth it.

CHAPTER 35

Nellie Dillon had meticulously planned the speech she was going to deliver to Brigit Barry, but as soon as she sat down in front of the girl, she was horrified that all the right words were coming out wrong.

"I gave your uncle what for, sending you down to a place like this. I asked the silly man, did he not know this is the twenty-first century? No, I take that back, he's not a silly man, sorry."

"It wasn't his fault I ended up here," Brigit explained. "Father Burns approached him…"

"Oh, did he now? The little weasel," Nellie cut in. She loathed the fellow in his black garb, which made his pale face look even paler, and as for his nose, it was like a vulture's beak. He sent shivers down her spine every time she saw him, and that wasn't often, because she didn't go to mass nowadays. Maybe when she would find herself at death's door, she would resume the practice in order to secure a place in heaven.

"It was a pity Father Scully died, he was really nice," Brigit remarked.

"Well, tell me about Father Burns," Nellie said.

"He told my uncle he knew of a couple down the country looking to adopt a child, and they were willing to pay big money."

"I thought all that stuff was done away with," Nellie said.

"Some things never change," Brigit said, smiling. "There are people who really want children and can't have them, and people who don't want children, having them."

"Please, don't tell me you've gone along with this adoption plan," Nellie said.

"The couple don't want to take him until he is a year old. They couldn't be putting up with screaming and crying at night, they said. They are paying for me to stay here, this is a posh place, I'll have you know." Brigit laughed nervously.

"Are you sure they are the kind of people who should take your child? Do they think everything will run smoothly when the child gets to be one? Do they think there will be no more tears? That's when the real trouble begins, silly idiots."

"They have a nursery here, and a nurse to look after the children. I am not the only one here, you know," Brigit said.

Nellie looked around the room, it was nice alright. Like a luxury hotel really. St. Hilda's Retreat was the name over the front door, she'd noticed on her way in.

"They should have a little plaque outside saying, 'We will do anything for money in St. Hilda's name'," Nellie said.

"You are here for what reason, Mrs Dillon?" Brigit prompted.

"I am here to do my duty," Nellie replied, smiling.

The tears that Brigit had held back up to now, started to flow.

"I am so sorry for what happened to your sons," Brigit said, sobbing.

"If you play with fire, you will get burned," Nellie replied. "And those two were striking matches from the day they were born. Although Pat wasn't a bad fellow, really, he wanted to be a priest. I'm glad he didn't get his wish because I never liked priests, would you believe," Nellie said.

Brigit was surprised to hear those unkind words about Dick, although not so much Pat, coming out of Mrs Dillon's mouth. She was their mother after all, and you were supposed to love your children; but, as the saying goes, if you want to know me, come and live with me. Love your children, that was a good one; she herself was a right hypocrite on that score. She wasn't going to love her child, she was going to sell him.

Brigit pulled herself together. "My uncle told me about Miss Kneeshaw killing your sons," she revealed.

Nellie held her tongue, she would not sully Miss Kneeshaw's name, not to anyone. People would expect her to be angry at what Miss Kneeshaw did, but she was not one bit angry, not angry at all.

"Dick was a right rogue, and you might find this hard to believe, but I did love him," Brigit admitted.

"I know exactly what you mean, I felt the same about his father," Nellie said, and smiled. "But, you know what? You can only give so much."

"I suppose you are right," Brigit said.

"Now, firstly, Brigit, let's get down to business. With regard to the child, you haven't signed anything yet, have you?" Nellie asked.

"There's no signing to be done, it is all to be done in secret, a kind of nudge-nudge, wink-wink thing," Brigit answered.

"Some things never change," Nellie said.

Brigit fought back the tears and managed to make a statement. "I am so confused. I thought it was going to be easy, but I am getting attached to the child, and I don't want to do that, because it will be so hard to let him go."

Nellie felt a sense of pride welling up inside her. Her son had done this young woman wrong, and she had a chance to atone for him.

"Tell me this, Brigit, would you like to return to Magnerstown?"

"No, I certainly would not. There are too many gossipmongers there. You know what I'd really love, though?" Brigit said.

"Tell me," Nellie said.

"I would love a fresh start, but that's impossible," Brigit said.

"Nothing is impossible." Nellie smiled.

"If only that were true," Brigit said.

"I have been doing a little bit of investigating myself. I would have made a great detective, much better that those two eejits in Magnerstown, who got the case solved for them by Miss Kneeshaw's confession," Nellie said with a wink. "Well, that's not entirely true, she didn't confess, but the thing she did to herself got them twigging that she had been involved in the three deaths. They are calling them the Keystone Cops in town, though the young fellow, James, is a clever fellow."

Brigit laughed. "Keystone cops, that's a good one," she said.

"There is a small pub for sale near here. I wouldn't mind a fresh start myself. I quite fancy being a landlord, or should I say landlady. You could run it for me, Brigit, and I could mind the little lad," Nellie said.

Tears welled up in Brigit's eyes.

"Miss Kneeshaw kindly left me some money. No, not some money, a lot of money, to be correct. She had her head screwed on, that one. So now I must put that money to good use. No point in having it languishing in a bank, is there?"

"Did I hear right, Miss Kneeshaw left you money?"

"Yes, Miss Kneeshaw, an angel in disguise. In fact, from now on I am going to think of her as my guardian angel."

"I can't let you do this."

"Course you can, you're owed it."

"But you're not responsible for your son's actions."

"I am responsible. I allowed Dick to turn out to be a brat, and he thought nothing of taking advantage of you."

"It takes two," Brigit said.

"No, he was always a sly scheming little so-and-so. I should have nipped it in the bud years ago. Chastised him when he needed it, by giving him a right good kick up his scrawny little arse."

Brigit laughed and cried at the same time.

"Now enough about Dick, the thing I want to know is, when am I going to see my grandchild?" Nellie said.

Brigit got up from her chair and rushed to Nellie. She threw her arms around the little woman and it felt so natural.

"If Miss Kneeshaw is your guardian angel, then you are mine," Brigit said, sobbing.

"That's a really lovely thing to say," Nellie whispered.

CHAPTER 36

Lilly knocked on James Sayder's hotel room door.

James ushered her in. "Lilly, lovely to see you. I was about to call on you, but you've saved me the trouble," he said.

Lilly noticed the open suitcase and the items of clothing neatly folded on the bed.

"That came out wrong," James said apologetically.

Lilly's heart sank. James was leaving, but why wouldn't he be doing so, considering there was nothing to keep him here now.

"So, how's your grandfather getting on? Still in hospital, is he?"

"Yes," Lilly whispered.

"He'll make a good recovery, don't worry. They have great treatment for heart trouble nowadays. Before you know it, he'll be back to his old self and back to where he belongs," James said.

Lilly burst into tears. James moved to her side and put his arm around her. Maybe he shouldn't have mentioned the man at all, but then if he didn't, she'd have thought him unfeeling.

Lilly plucked a tissue from her pocket and dabbed her eyes. "He has lost the will to live, and it's all over her," Lilly said.

James pushed the suitcase aside. "Sit down there," he said.

Lilly gathered herself and sat down on the vacant space on the bed.

"Take a few deep breaths and you'll be fine," James suggested.

"It'll take more than a few deep breaths, I am afraid, for me to be fine," Lilly said.

James jerked his head in the direction of the tray containing a kettle, sachets of tea, coffee, sugar and little pots of long-life milk. A bottle of still water stood in all its glory beside the kettle, because James never trusted the water that came out of hotel taps. "Would you like a cup of tea?" he said.

"I want to tell you this before I lose my bottle," Lilly said.

"Alright, I'm listening," James said.

"He just wants to die because she's gone," Lilly said.

"His wife?" James asked.

"No, the jeweller woman," Lilly said.

"You mean Miss Kneeshaw?"

"I didn't know he knew her so well. He really kept that a secret," Lilly snapped.

"But what's so wrong with that?" James asked.

"There's something I should tell you," Lilly said. "The only thing is, I will feel like a bit of a traitor if I do."

James put a finger to his lips and pointed in the direction of next door.

"The walls have ears," he whispered.

Lilly got the message and stopped talking.

James steered Lilly towards the door. "Some people have microphonic ears, if you get my drift," he whispered.

Lilly knew it was Robert Carroll who occupied the room next door.

"Let me have a farewell drink with you in the bar," James suggested.

"That would be nice," Lilly agreed. "But would you mind if I went home to do a few bits and pieces? I could meet you in an hour."

"That would suit me," James said. "I could finish my packing and then I won't have it hanging over me."

"I'll send you a text," Lilly said.

"Great. Look forward to it." James smiled.

CHAPTER 37

Lilly sat beside James in the hotel lobby. How was she going to word this? Just start at the beginning would be the best way forward, she concluded.

"There's something my grandfather told me, and I feel it is my duty to tell you, but I don't want to," Lilly said.

"Well, if it isn't the lovely Lilly Larby. Is this your young man? You are such a sly old thing, if you don't mind me saying so, Lilly."

Lilly stared at the figure towering above her.

"I'm here to meet Detective Inspector Carroll. I've notes to write up for him," the larger-than-life woman said.

James was amused. The desk sergeant was obviously having a laugh.

Lilly looked James in the face. "This is Celine," she said.

Realization dawned on James. The absentee secretary who was holidaying in Spain was now here, in the flesh. "I heard all about you," he said.

"All good, I hope," Celine said, smiling.

"This is James Sayder, Robert Carroll's assistant," Lilly said.

"I think the desk sergeant is playing an April Fool's Day joke on you," James said.

"It's not April Fool's Day," Celine said, and laughed.

"Every day in this town is April Fool's Day," Lilly said bitterly.

"Right, I'll toddle off to the leisure centre for a tanning session. Have to keep it up, otherwise all that toasting out in Spain will have been for nothing. You should go there, Lilly, you'd love it."

"Nice to have met you," James said.

"I've a dinner engagement to go to tonight," Celine said, and winked.

"Cliff's Restaurant?" James asked.

"A private sitting," Celine said, and laughed. "I feel like chicken tonight," she hummed.

"Nice one," James said.

"It's been marinating all day in his fridge, and let's hope that's the only thing that has been marinating." Celine gave a dirty laugh and then left.

"So, that was the infamous Celine, and she's having chicken tonight." James laughed. It had to be Doctor Morris she was meeting. He was probably trying out his spatchcock recipe on every available woman in town.

"She's like a massive bubble," Lilly said.

"Listen, Lilly, there's something I want to say," James said.

Lilly leaned back on the chair and closed her eyes.

"You don't have to tell me anything at all. It would serve no purpose, if you get my meaning. If you don't mind a bit of advice, Lilly, I think you should spend as much time with your grandfather as you can, because you will miss him when he is gone," James said.

Lilly stared at James.

"Not that he will be gone any time soon, he will make a good recovery, I am sure of it."

"I hope you are right, James."

"You should only be thinking about the good things. Trust me, Lilly, I know what I'm talking about," James said.

"Thank you, James," Lilly whispered. "Thank you so much."

"You will keep in touch now, won't you, Lilly?"

Lilly studied the young man she had grown to look upon with fondness, but he was never going to be hers, she knew.

He had that faraway look in his eye, and she knew someone else had got there first.

* * *

Robert threw his possessions at his suitcase. He wasn't one bit pleased that the case was over. Someone helped that jeweller woman to dispose of the bodies. He should have found out who that person was and charged them with accessory to murder. Accessory to three murders to be correct.

Miss Kneeshaw did the killings, yes, that was a true. Everyone in town was now in possession of this information, but nobody seemed to be questioning how she disposed of the bodies. He had even bought *The Crier* just to see if Mossie Harrington had hammered out an article suggesting an old woman could not be capable of dumping the bodies into the well, and why was that helper getting away scot-free? It would be such a great opportunity for the brave Mossie to have yet another dig at the investigation.

Robert almost didn't hear the knock on the door with the steam that was coming out of his ears.

It's probably housekeeping, he guessed. That's how the young woman introduced herself each and every morning.

Do you want your room serviced, she would ask, but today she would not be offering that service, because he was leaving, wasn't he? You can service it for the next person who will probably be along in six months' time, he would love to say to her.

On the other hand, she may only be here to inform him that twelve o'clock is the checking out time. He was glad to be getting out of the tomb that was so badly in need of updating; in fact, the only answer was to gut the place and build it back up from scratch. He was surprised the owner hadn't applied for a grant to do it up. They were throwing grants out nowadays like smarties. Martin Hayes could do with the work now that the job out at the well was no more, seeing Counsellor Hanton had met his Waterloo, or would some other official busybody take it over?

Robert called out in answer to the second knock, which sounded louder than the one before. "Keep your wig on, I'm coming."

He didn't fully open the door just in case the eager-to-clean-for-the-nation woman with her brushes, bottles, cloths, and potions, burst into the room.

"I'll be out in an hour, if you would have the decency to let me get on with my packing," Robert said frostily.

"You will not be out in an hour. I have told them downstairs to leave your booking open until further notice," the voice from the other side of the door said.

Robert threw open the door and stared in disbelief at the woman standing there.

"We have things to do, a man to be reinstalled in his house, so I can have Forge Cottage back, and that's just for starters."

"Maggie," Robert croaked.

If you enjoyed this book, please let others know by leaving a quick review on Amazon. Also, if you spot anything untoward in the paperback, get in touch. We strive for the best quality and appreciate reader feedback.

editor@thebookfolks.com

www.thebookfolks.com

Also by Anne Crosse

If you enjoyed this book and you haven't already, check out the other titles in the series:

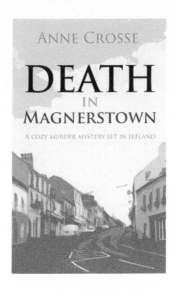

ANNE CROSSE

DEATH
IN
MAGNERSTOWN

A COZY MURDER MYSTERY SET IN IRELAND

BOOK 1

A judge is found dead in his courthouse. A bigwig in a small Irish town, the pressure is on to find answers. But quite a few people wanted the hardliner out of their lives. The regional newspaper always seems to know more than the police. With the chief inspector and the publisher at loggerheads, will the culprit ever be found?

Available FREE with Kindle Unlimited and in paperback.

BOOK 3

A storm brews over the Irish village of Magnerstown when a recycling plant worker discovers human body parts. Detective Robert Carroll leads the investigation, but his focus is more on his next drink. Sidekick James Sayder takes the reins, and closes in on the culprits.

Available FREE with Kindle Unlimited and in paperback.

Made in the USA
Monee, IL
13 November 2020

47481362R00111